WATCH OUT, REVA!

Danny took a deep breath, then another.

Reva, where are you? he asked silently, leaning out from behind the tall packing crate.

And then there she was.

He crept up behind her.

He raised the black wool coat.

I've got you now, he thought, struggling against the rage that roared through every muscle.

I've got you now, Reva.

I hope I don't have to do anything terrible.

Books by R. L. Stine

Fear Street

THE NEW GIRL
THE SURPRISE PARTY
THE OVERNIGHT
MISSING
THE WRONG NUMBER
THE SLEEPWALKER
HAUNTED
HALLOWEEN PARTY
THE STEPSISTER
SKI WEEKEND
THE FIRE GAME
LIGHTS OUT
THE SECRET BEDROOM
THE KNIFE
PROM QUEEN
FIRST DATE
THE BEST FRIEND
THE CHEATER
SUNBURN
THE NEW BOY
THE DARE
BAD DREAMS
DOUBLE DATE
THE THRILL CLUB
ONE EVIL SUMMER

Fear Street Super Chiller

PARTY SUMMER
SILENT NIGHT
GOODNIGHT KISS
BROKEN HEARTS
SILENT NIGHT 2
THE DEAD LIFEGUARD

The Fear Street Saga

THE BETRAYAL
THE SECRET
THE BURNING

Fear Street Cheerleaders

THE FIRST EVIL
THE SECOND EVIL
THE THIRD EVIL

99 Fear Street: The House of Evil

THE FIRST HORROR
THE SECOND HORROR
THE THIRD HORROR

Other Novels

HOW I BROKE UP WITH ERNIE
PHONE CALLS
CURTAINS
BROKEN DATE

Available from ARCHWAY Paperbacks

FEAR STREET®

SUPER CHILLER

R·L·STINE

Silent Night 2

AN ARCHWAY PAPERBACK
Published by POCKET BOOKS
New York London Toronto Sydney Tokyo Singapore

This book is a work of fiction. Names, characters, places and incidents are either products of the author's imagination or are used fictitiously. Any resemblance to actual events or locales or persons, living or dead, is entirely coincidental.

AN ARCHWAY PAPERBACK *Original*

An Archway Paperback published by
POCKET BOOKS, a division of Simon & Schuster Inc.
1230 Avenue of the Americas, New York, NY 10020

ISBN: 0-671-78619-9

First Archway Paperback printing December 1993

10 9 8 7 6 5 4

Cover art by Bill Schmidt

Printed in the U.S.A.

IL 6+

PART ONE

A KIDNAPPING

Chapter 1

HOLIDAY PLANS

Paul Nichols felt like killing someone.

He tapped both hands against the steering wheel and waited for the light to change. The stoplight glared at him, reflecting his anger, until the icy street and snow-covered trees and bushes seemed to glow red through the clouded windshield. Angry red.

The soft, familiar melody of "Silent Night" came on the radio, and he grabbed the dial and turned the music off with a bitter groan.

Less than two weeks before Christmas, Paul thought, staring into the red glow of the traffic light. Cold air blew over his feet from the broken heater. Why did he even bother to turn it on?

Nearly Christmas and he had no job. No money. No *nothing.*

"M-Merry Christmas to me," he muttered under his breath. His stammer was back. It always came back when he was angry or tense.

The light changed. He floored the gas pedal, and the old Plymouth squealed into the intersection, the smooth tires spinning over the ice.

He had to slow down as he reached the center of town. Waynesbridge was known as "Christmas Town" because of its lavish decorations, which included a brightly decorated Christmas tree on every corner of Main Street.

The shimmering lights only darkened Paul's mood. He slowed to a stop, allowing a family of four to cross the street. They were smiling, their faces red beneath their wool ski caps. The two kids were pointing to the window of Toy Village, the big toy store on the corner.

Watching the father take the little boy's hand as they crossed, Paul thought of his family. Christmas was supposed to be a family time, after all.

But not for Paul. He hadn't seen his parents since he was sixteen, two years earlier. Not since he had dropped out of Waynesbridge High in his junior year.

"Hope they have a r-rotten Christmas," he muttered, squeezing the steering wheel harder until both hands ached.

A few minutes later he parked the car at the curb in front of his apartment building and climbed out. The late-afternoon sky was scarlet, the red ball of a sun lowering behind the two-story brick building. Paul's sneakers crunched over the small piles of hard, dirty snow as he jogged around to the back.

The metal stairs clanged beneath him as he made his way to his apartment on the second floor. Shivering beneath his brown leather bomber jacket, he pushed open the door and stepped inside.

"Hey—!" Diane Morris glanced up in surprise. She made no attempt to rise from the green vinyl couch.

Paul's expression remained blank. "Diane, you here?"

She let the copy of *People* drop from her hand. "Yeah. You don't mind, do you, Pres? My mom and dad—they're tearing into each other, for a change. They're both so drunk, it's disgusting. I couldn't stay there."

Paul grunted in reply. He tossed his jacket onto a chair and crossed the small room. An open bag of potato chips lay on the counter that separated the living room from the narrow kitchenette. He picked it up and stuffed a handful of chips into his mouth.

"Did you get the job, Pres?" Diane asked, sitting up.

He shook his head.

Her hopeful expression faded. She lowered her eyes to the floor. "What about the one at Pick and Pay?"

"I'm not going to deliver groceries!" he exploded, slamming the potato chip bag down on the counter. "I'm n-not a delivery boy!"

"Okay. Okay, Pres," she replied softly. She crossed the room to give him a long, tender kiss. He pulled away impatiently, turning his back on her.

"Pres?" Diane pretended to be hurt. She had

been going with him for three years. She was used to his outbursts. "Let me see your sneer," she asked, teasing. "Come on. Let me see it."

He could never stay angry at her. He curled his lip and turned, giving her his best sneer.

Diane called him Pres because he reminded her of Elvis Presley. He had the same straight black hair, which he wore with long sideburns. He had Elvis Presley's dark, romantic eyes. And he had the Elvis sneer, which she had once caught him practicing in front of a mirror.

She laughed. "You could be a star, Pres. You really could."

"You're really stupid, Diane." He said it with a smile.

"Yeah. Because I hang around with you," she shot back. She stuck her tongue out at him.

Diane rubbed her skinny arms through the thin pink sweater she wore over straight-legged black denim jeans. The light from the table lamp caught her white-blond hair, tied back with a pink band. The black roots formed a dark, jagged line along her forehead.

She studied Paul with her gray-blue eyes, her best feature. Before she had become a blonde, she had always thought of herself as mousy and plain. She was especially self-conscious about her two front teeth, which poked out. She *hated* it when Pres called her Rabbit. He did it only when he wanted to annoy her.

Diane was seventeen, a year younger than Pres. She had graduated from Waynesbridge High the previous June with a solid C average. She could have gotten better grades, but it was impossible to study at home since her parents were always drunk, always fighting. She spent most of her time at Pres's shabby apartment.

She hadn't been able to find a job either.

"Oh, sigh," she declared, shaking her head. She dropped down on the couch. The vinyl cushion made a loud *whoosh.* She raised her eyes to his. "*Now* what are we going to do? Did you see any other ads in the paper?"

Pres shook his head. He carried the bag of potato chips over to the couch and sat down next to her. He stared at the bag as if studying it.

"Well, we're broke," Diane continued. She poked him in the ribs. "How are you going to buy that Jaguar you promised me?"

He sneered. "Don't make me laugh."

Diane bent to pick up the magazine. "I was just reading about a man and a woman who robbed an armored truck. You know, one of those little trucks that carries money from banks. They parked their car so that it blocked off the street and pretended to have a flat. When the armored truck stopped, they both pulled out automatic weapons. They got six million dollars."

Pres shook his head. "Wow. Good work!"

"Maybe we could do that," Diane suggested seriously.

Diane had fantasies that the two of them would become big-time criminals. She was always coming up with schemes in which they performed wild, daring robberies, just like in the movies, and got away with millions.

At first Pres had thought she was joking, making up stories to amuse herself. After a while he realized that Diane was serious. She really believed they could get rich by pulling off a major crime.

"What have we got to lose?" she asked. A familiar question. That's what she always asked: "What have we got to lose?"

"Well, I've already lost one job," he replied bitterly, his fingers playing with a tear in the vinyl on the arm of the couch.

Pres thought about the job he had for nearly two years at Dalby's Department Store. Being a stockroom clerk wasn't exactly a glamorous job. But the pay was enough to live on. And from time to time he had been able to steal some nice items—a leather bomber jacket, a watch, a portable TV.

Not a bad job at all.

But then one of the security guards had caught him with a portable cassette player under his jacket—and that was the end of the job.

Pres had been taken to Robert Dalby himself. *Dalby himself!* Dalby liked to lecture employees caught stealing before he fired them.

What a jerk!

Pres had been so angry, he couldn't even stammer out an excuse. Dalby's face turned red, bright red. And Pres had to hold himself back, had to keep his hands stuffed tightly in his jeans pockets, had to fight off the impulse to grab Dalby by the throat, to strangle him with his own silk necktie.

Pres hadn't been able to find another job. It had been nearly three months. Three months of anger and rejection.

Diane's voice broke into his bitter thoughts. He realized she had been talking to him, but he hadn't heard a word.

"So?" she asked impatiently. "Did you?"

"Did I what?" Pres asked. The potato chip bag was empty. He crinkled it into a ball and tossed it across the room.

"Did you scout out Dalby's house?" Diane demanded, her eyes narrowed at him, questioning him.

"Yeah, I checked it out," he told her.

"And?"

"And it wouldn't be hard to get in there," he said without enthusiasm.

"Really?" Diane grabbed his hand and squeezed it excitedly.

"I saw one guard dog. That's all," Pres told her.

"You really think we could get in?" Diane demanded, holding on to his hand.

"Piece of cake." He turned to study her face. "Hey, you're really serious about this? About robbing Dalby's house?"

"Don't I *look* serious?" she replied. "It's the perfect revenge, isn't it, Pres?"

He frowned. "Not if we get caught."

He flashed back three months and felt the store security guard's hand on his shoulder. Once again he saw everyone in the store staring at him, staring as he was dragged up to Dalby's sixth-floor office to be fired.

"You were in Dalby's house once, right?" Diane asked, lost in her own thoughts. "You saw the stuff in there?"

"Yeah. It was last winter. Some kind of store party," Pres replied. "The place is loaded with antiques."

Diane is really serious about this, he realized again.

Am I serious about it?

He wasn't sure.

"We could do it, Pres," Diane said excitedly, squeezing his hand. "We could pay Dalby back for firing you. We could get in there and grab enough antiques to make sure we have a *great* Christmas! I mean, we could have a tree and presents and a turkey dinner—and *everything!*"

With a burst of enthusiasm she wrapped her arms around his shoulders and kissed him. Her lips felt hot against his. "We could do it!" she cried. "It would be just like a movie, Pres. Just like a movie!"

She held him tightly, her thin body trembling with excitement. "What do you say?"

He stared across the room. His eyes moved from the shabby furniture to the threadbare carpet.

Then, in a quick, sudden movement, he stood up. He turned and stared at her, a smile breaking out on his handsome face. "I have a better idea," he said.

"Huh?" Diane gaped up at him, her mouth hanging open.

"Forget the antiques," Pres told her with a sneer. "What do *we* know about antiques? Nothing."

"Yes, but—" Diane started to say.

He raised a hand to silence her. "What is Dalby's most precious possession?"

Diane shrugged. "How should I know?"

"His daughter!" Pres declared.

"Reva," Diane murmured, surprised she remembered the name. "Reva Dalby."

"Right," Pres said. "How much could we get for antiques? A few thousand maybe? Maybe. But Dalby will fork over *millions* for his daughter."

Diane chewed tensely on her lower lip. Her gray-blue eyes locked on Pres. "You mean—?"

"Yes!" Pres declared. "Y-you want a movie? It'll be just like a movie, Diane! We just have to work it out carefully, step by step. Scene by scene. And with a little luck . . ." He grinned excitedly at her. "With a little luck we could be *millionaires* by Christmas! All we have to do is kidnap Reva Dalby."

Chapter 2

REVA IS CAPTURED

Reva Dalby backed up to the railing and raised her hands as if to shield herself. The dark figure continued to move toward her, advancing slowly, steadily.

She let out a soft cry.

The department store was dark and empty, silent except for the chorus singing "Silent Night" on the speaker system.

The man drew closer. He was breathing hard, each breath a menacing groan.

Reva pressed her back against the low chrome balcony railing. She glanced down to the main floor of the department store, shadowy and still, five floors below. She stared at the enormous Christmas tree twinkling brightly in the center aisle. Another chorus of "Silent Night" jarred the eerie quiet.

"Please—no!" she cried to her attacker.

He had a pistol in one hand.

He leapt at her, arms outstretched.

She shut her eyes and ducked.

She could feel a cold gust of wind as he sailed over her, sailed over the balcony.

She could hear him scream all the way down.

Then she heard shattering glass. A loud crack.

And then a long, tortured scream as her attacker landed on the Christmas tree. It shorted out. He twisted and writhed in the blue-white electrical current.

Zapzapzapzap.

The stinging hiss of death. A sound Reva knew she'd never forget.

And then she heard his thin voice. He was saying, "Excuse me, miss. Miss?"

Zapzapzapzap.

"Excuse me, miss," he was saying. "Can you help me?"

Reva blinked. She realized she wasn't up on the balcony. She was behind the perfume counter on the first floor. Slowly, she left the past and the scene she had pictured again and again since the Christmas before.

Now it was a year later. One year later, and she still thought about that horrifying night every time she heard "Silent Night" over the store's sound system.

She couldn't help but remember.

"Can you help me, miss?" The voice finally cut all the way through her thoughts.

She was facing a middle-aged man with thinning

gray hair. He was wearing a brown overcoat and carrying a worn leather briefcase. From the impatient frown on his face, she could tell he had been trying to get her attention for some time.

"Do you work here?" he asked, staring at her with gray watery eyes.

"No. I just like to stand behind the counter," Reva replied, rolling her eyes. Cold blue eyes that grew colder as she gazed at the man's threadbare overcoat.

"Could you help me choose a perfume?" he asked, staring down at the shiny glass bottles inside the display case.

"For *you?"* Reva demanded with a scornful laugh.

The man blushed. "No. Of course not. For my wife."

"Sorry. I'm on my break." Reva turned away from him. She lowered her gaze to an oval mirror on the counter and began pushing at her wavy red hair with one hand.

"On your break? But the store just opened!" the man declared, his face growing even redder.

Reva didn't look up from the mirror. "I don't make the schedules," she said. She stared at his face in the mirror, enjoying his angry, helpless expression. She had to struggle to keep from laughing aloud.

The man took a deep breath. "Listen, miss, couldn't you help me? You seem to be the only salesperson in this department. I've got to be at work in ten minutes."

"Sorry. Store rules," Reva replied, yawning into her hand.

"But, really—"

Reva turned to face him. Her eyes rolled scornfully over his unstylish brown overcoat, his shabby briefcase. "You'd probably do better in the bargain basement," she told him. "The stairs are right over there." She pointed.

The man uttered an exasperated cry. He angrily jerked his briefcase off the counter and stormed toward the exit.

What is his problem? Reva asked herself, laughing. I was just trying to help the poor geek save a little money.

Reva's laughter was cut short by someone noisily clearing her throat behind her. Reva turned to see Arlene Smith, the cosmetics department supervisor, glaring at her disapprovingly, her bony arms crossed tightly in front of her gray suit jacket.

"Reva, you were inexcusably rude to that customer," Ms. Smith, as she liked to be called, said through clenched teeth.

"He'll probably survive," Reva replied dryly.

"But will the *store* survive?" Ms. Smith demanded angrily.

Reva rolled her eyes. "I'm sorry, Ms. Smith," she said, emphasizing the *Ms.* "But you really shouldn't get on my case just because you're having a bad hair day!"

Ms. Smith narrowed her eyes menacingly. "I'm going to talk to your father about this, Reva. Your attitude has not improved."

"I wish you *would* talk to him," Reva said with a sigh. "I didn't want to come back to the store this Christmas. But my father made me. He said it would be good for me."

"I don't think it's good for any of us," Ms. Smith replied huffily. She made her way across the department, taking angry strides, her high heels clicking on the hard floor.

Where did she get those shoes? At a blacksmith's? Reva asked herself, chuckling.

She raised her hands and examined her nails. They were long and perfect, and the night before she had coated them with a new shade of purple. Just for fun she had put a black dot in the center of each nail. She knew it would drive Ms. Smith crazy.

Even though it was early, not yet ten o'clock, the store had begun to fill up with eager Christmas shoppers. Reva watched a very plump woman across the aisle trying to squeeze between two racks of pocketbooks. "How about eating a *salad* once in a while!" she called to the woman, knowing she couldn't be heard over the din.

Reva reached under the counter and pulled up the tall bottle of Evian water she kept there. She took a sip, then stopped when she saw a familiar figure loping down the aisle toward her. Kyle Storer. The usual grin on his face.

Kyle thought he was so hot. He had been hitting on Reva ever since school vacation had started and they both began working at Dalby's. But she had refused to go out with him.

Why? He was too eager.

Now here he was, coming to try again. Reva groaned to herself, watching him approach, his green eyes twinkling. Kyle wore tan chinos over black boots, and a blue- and white-checked western-style shirt with a navy blue string tie.

Cute. Real cute, Reva thought scornfully. What a cowboy. Maybe he's coming over here to yodel.

"Hey—whussup?" Kyle asked, his grin growing wider. "Whussup, Reva?"

"What are you supposed to be?" Reva asked, staring at his string tie.

Kyle's grin faded. "Huh? You mean my tie? You like it?"

"I'm kind of busy," Reva said. "Hint-hint."

Kyle ignored her cold reception. "The store's really crowded already," he said, glancing around. "Guess your dad is raking it in today, huh?" He laughed as if he had just made a joke.

"Kyle, I really can't talk," Reva insisted. "I already got in trouble with Ms. Smith this morning."

Why can't he take a hint? Reva wondered. If he asks me out again, he's going to be sorry.

"You doing anything Saturday night?" Kyle asked, leaning over the glass counter.

Reva shot her hand out, tipping over the bottle of Evian water. "Oh! I'm sorry!" she cried, watching the water spill down the front of Kyle's chinos.

Kyle took a step back, his mouth dropping open as he saw the big wet stain on the front of his pants.

"How embarrassing!" Reva cried with mock sympathy. "Kyle, what will the customers think?"

Kyle shrugged and tried to act cool, but his face was bright red. "Later," he mumbled, and hurried away.

When she finished laughing, Reva took a long drink from the Evian bottle. Then she turned to see Francine, the frizzy-haired, mousy woman who shared the perfume-counter duties, step up beside her, shaking her head. "Sorry I'm late, Reva. My car broke down in the middle of Division Street. Has it been terribly busy?"

"Yes, terribly," Reva replied, sighing. "I'm exhausted already, Francine. I'm going to take my break. See you."

Francine tried to sputter a protest. But Reva ignored her and hurried down the aisle.

As she passed by the Christmas tree, Reva felt a cold chill on the back of her neck. Once again memories of last Christmas and all its horror forced their way into her mind.

I promised I'd be a kinder person after all that happened last Christmas, Reva remembered. I promised I'd be nicer, warmer, more considerate.

Well, I *would* be nicer if I were lying in a bikini on a hot beach somewhere! she told herself. I'd be a *lot* nicer, that's for sure!

But how can I be nice if I have to spend Christmas vacation standing behind a perfume counter, waiting on tacky jerks in this stuffy store?

Reva made her way past the stocking department, headed down three steps, and spotted her cousin Pam beside a long wall of greeting cards.

Pam had red and green ribbons in her straight

blond hair. She wore a short green skirt over red tights and a red stretch top.

I knew I could count on Pam to have plenty of Christmas spirit, Reva thought sarcastically. I guess she's happy just to have a job.

Pam's mother had been laid off most of the year. And her father had to give up his drugstore and go to work for someone else.

But, thought Reva, Cousin Pam seems as bright and cheery as ever.

And who is that *babe* she's talking to?

As Reva entered the stationery department, she saw that Pam had her hand on the shoulder of a dark, very handsome boy in black denims and a white sweater. He had straight black hair pulled back in a short ponytail, a broad, tanned forehead, and intense dark eyes that were locked on Pam. He was smiling at Pam, the most beautiful smile Reva had ever seen.

"Hi, guys," Reva said, stepping between Pam and the boy. Pam was forced to remove her hand from his shoulder and take a step back. "How's life in the stationery department, Pam?" Reva asked, her eyes on the boy.

"Great!" Pam replied. "It's an easy job. Not bad at all."

"Way to go," Reva said. She still hadn't taken her eyes from the boy.

"Have you—uh—met Victor?" Pam asked. "This is Victor Dias. My cousin Reva."

"Hi." Victor gave Reva a shy smile.

Wow, Reva thought. What a smile! What a *babe!*

I am totally *captured* by this guy, Reva told herself.

"Do you work in the store?" Reva asked, returning his smile, training her blue eyes on his.

"Yes. For the holiday," Victor replied. "In the stockroom, usually."

"The stockroom? I have to work there every day from three to five," Reva said. She absolutely hated working in the stockroom. But now, she thought, studying Victor's handsome face, maybe she'd enjoy it a lot more.

"Do you like it here?" she asked him, eager to keep the conversation going.

"Be careful, Victor," Pam broke in. "Reva's father owns all the Dalby stores."

Victor smiled. "I *love* working in the stockroom. I hope to work there all my life!" he joked.

Reva laughed.

Victor glanced at his watch. "I'd better get back. See you later, Pam." He turned to leave.

"I work in the perfume department," Reva called after him. "Come say hi sometime, okay?"

"Nice to meet you," Victor called over his shoulder. He disappeared into the crowd of shoppers.

"Isn't he terrific?" Pam gushed.

Reva finally faced her cousin. "Seems like a good guy," she said casually.

Pam's face was flushed. Her green eyes flashed excitedly. "I think this is the real thing, Reva," she whispered, grinning. "I mean, I met Victor only a few weeks ago. But I . . . well . . . I'm just nuts about him."

"That's great, Pam," Reva replied without any

emotion, as if Pam had just told her it was cloudy outside or something just as dull. She raised the backs of her hands to her cousin. "How do you like my nails?"

"Huh?" Pam seemed confused by the sudden change of subject.

"Will these drive Ms. Smith wild, or what?" Reva demanded, holding the black-dotted purple fingernails in Pam's face.

To Reva's surprise, Pam reached down and picked up a silver-bladed letter opener from a stationery display. Pam raised the letter opener high.

"Pam—what's that?" Reva cried.

"Here's what I think of your nails!" Pam exclaimed. And she plunged the letter opener into Reva's chest.

Chapter 3

GRABBED

Reva uttered a choked gasp.

Pam laughed.

She raised the letter opener and pushed the blade two or three more times into Reva's chest. "Gotcha," Pam cried, her green eyes sparkling with excitement in the bright store light.

Reva took a step back, her eyes still wide with fear. She stared at the fake letter opener, realizing that it had a sliding blade. The blade slid into the handle when it was pressed against anything.

Still grinning, Pam pushed the blade into the palm of one hand. "Do you believe this joke letter opener is the biggest seller in the stationery department this Christmas?" Pam declared, shaking her head.

"It's . . . very funny," Reva said weakly. "Glad you're having fun, Pam."

"It beats last Christmas," Pam remarked, eyeing Reva meaningfully.

"For sure," Reva muttered.

Reva said goodbye to her cousin. Then she walked as slowly as she could back to the perfume counter, thinking about Victor.

After work Reva made her way up to the executive offices on the sixth floor to meet her father. She passed the luxurious reception area with its leather couches, fresh flowers in tall glass vases, and fabric-covered walls studded with modern paintings.

Following the hall to her father's office in the corner, Reva paused as the balcony came into view. The balcony from which she could look down on all five floors to the first one. The balcony where she had almost met her death.

Feeling a cold shiver down her back, Reva held her breath and jogged the rest of the way, her eyes straight ahead.

Mr. Dalby was standing in the doorway to his office, a stack of files in his hands. He smiled as Reva approached. "How's it going?"

Reva's father was a trim, handsome man who worked out every day and took very good care of himself. He was forty-six but appeared younger. The only signs of age were the creases at the corners of his dark eyes and the sweeping trails of gray on the sides of his black, closely trimmed hair.

"How's it going? Not great," Reva complained.

She followed her father into his office and sat down in front of his wide blond-wood desk.

She turned the photo in the Plexiglas frame on the corner of the desk to peek at it. She had seen it at least a thousand times, but it still made her feel sad. It was a snapshot of Reva, her little brother, Michael, and their mother on the beach at the Cape. It had been taken five years earlier, just six months before Reva's mother had died.

What a photo, she thought, turning it back. So happy and so sad at the same time. She always wondered how her father could bear to keep it in front of him all day.

Mr. Dalby sat in his chair and leaned over his desk, studying Reva's face. "Ms. Smith complained about you this morning," he murmured.

Reva shrugged, as if to say who cares. "I really don't want to work here this Christmas, Daddy," she said, not meaning to sound as whiny as she did. "I mean, it's not like we need the money."

Mr. Dalby frowned. He tapped a pencil on the desktop as he continued to stare at her thoughtfully. "I really want you to work," he said softly. "For your own good, Reva. I know it brings back bad memories. But I feel you have to get over them."

"I really need a rest, that's all," Reva insisted. "Why can't I go to Saint Croix with Michael?"

"Because the Harrisons didn't invite you," her father answered bluntly. "They only invited your brother."

Reva blew a strand of red hair off her forehead. "Bummer," she muttered.

"Tell you what," Mr. Dalby said, tossing down

the pencil. His expression brightened. "Stick it out here in the store this Christmas, and we'll go somewhere warm in February."

"Really?" Reva pulled herself up from her slouching position in the chair. Her blue eyes brightened.

"And you can take a friend along," he added. "You can't get a better offer than that."

Reva laughed. "Is this what you might call a bribe?"

Mr. Dalby nodded. "Yes. It's definitely a bribe."

Reva jumped up, leaned over the desk, and kissed his cheek.

His dark eyes grew wide with surprise. He wasn't used to receiving much affection from his daughter.

"Okay, so I'm letting you bribe me," Reva said, smiling. "I love being bribed, actually."

"And you'll keep the job in the store?" he demanded.

"Yeah. Sure," Reva replied.

"And I won't get any more complaints from Ms. Smith that you're being rude to the customers?" he asked, raising his eyebrows.

"Hey—don't expect miracles!" Reva exclaimed. She started to walk over to the coat closet against the wall. "Are you coming home?"

Mr. Dalby sighed and pointed to the stack of files on his desk. "I can't. I have to work late. I have all these inventory reports to go over."

Reva pulled on her coat. "Okay. See you later." She stopped at the door. "Thanks for the bribe, Daddy."

"Any time."

Humming to herself, Reva made her way down the hallway toward the two service elevators that were for store employees. Most of the offices she passed were empty. The desks out front were empty too. The secretaries went home promptly at five.

Her voice sounded hollow in the silent hallway. She stopped humming.

She didn't like being out there all alone.

Feeling her heart pound harder, Reva stepped up to one of the employees' elevators. The doors were shiny aluminum. She could see her reflection in them. Two Revas stared back at her, slightly distorted, both a little anxious, a little frightened.

She pushed the button.

The doors to the elevator to her left slid open.

She started toward it.

But a loud voice behind her uttered a sharp cry.

And strong hands grabbed her arms from behind.

Chapter 4

REVA IS AFRAID

Reva felt herself being dragged back.

With a desperate burst of strength she jerked herself free and spun around.

"Huh? Daddy?" she cried.

"Don't use the employees' elevators," he told her, watching the doors slide shut. "I've been having trouble with both of them. I've had the company working on them."

"Daddy—you frightened me!" Reva exclaimed.

He was panting loudly. He had run all the way down the hall to stop her. "I'm sorry, Reva. They could be dangerous. They were supposed to put a sign up."

"Wow!" Reva exclaimed. "Wow." Her heartbeat was slowly returning to normal. "It's never dull around here."

She said goodbye to her father once again and made her way to the bank of main elevators. She rode down to the first floor, covering her ears to shut out the *rum-tum-tums* of "The Little Drummer Boy" playing over the elevator loudspeaker.

The store had been closed for nearly half an hour. The blue-uniformed cleaning people were noisily hauling out their mops, buckets, and enormous vacuum cleaners. Several floor managers were rearranging shelves.

Reva hurried through the aisles to the employees' exit. The store always gave her the creeps after the customers had left. The air was too still. The aisles too empty. The mannequins all seemed to be staring at her.

There were too many frightening memories. . . .

Zipping her coat, she stepped out into a clear, cold evening. The violet sky sparkled with a thousand tiny stars.

Her blue Dr. Martens thudded against the concrete as she made her way across the wide loading dock and down the shallow steps. A gust of wind rattled the chain-link fence that surrounded the asphalt lot. Fat brown leaves scrabbled against the fence as if trying to break through.

Why does the employee parking lot have to be so far from the store? Reva wondered. She raised the collar of her coat and began to jog. It's so dark back here, she thought with a shiver. It wouldn't kill Daddy to put up a few lights.

The gate at the end of the loading area came dimly into view. Beyond the gate stretched a narrow alleyway between two buildings. The parking lot stood at the end of the alley.

Reva stepped through the gate and made her way quickly through the narrow passageway. The two buildings formed tall, dark walls on both sides of her.

Her shoes crunched over broken glass and old snow. The wind whistled through the alley, pushed against her as if trying to drive her back.

She was about halfway through the dark tunnel when she heard the footsteps.

Behind her.

Slow at first, then picking up speed.

Reva's breath caught in her throat. The wind howled. She could hear the footsteps over the wind.

Closer. Closer.

More than one person.

She froze. Then forced her legs to move.

Gripping her coat collar with both hands, she lowered her head against the wind and ran.

Gray light shimmered at the end of the alley. Reva ran toward the light. She nearly tripped over an empty Coke can. It clattered noisily, bouncing over the asphalt.

The footsteps were close behind.

How many people were there? How many people were chasing her?

She didn't turn around. She kept her head lowered against the whistling wind. The gray light opened like a mist at the end of the passageway.

She gasped for breath, running at full speed. Running to the light.

The rows of cars came into view as she stepped out of the darkness. The lot stretched in front of her. White light from tall poles bounced off the cars like bright comets.

Reva spotted her new red Miata alone by the fence in the first row.

If I can get there, I'll be safe, she thought. Safe . . .

Safe from whom?

Who could be chasing her? And why?

Without slowing, she turned her head.

And recognized the man and woman.

Two sales managers from the store. They waved good night to each other and hurried across the lot to their cars.

Reva stopped a few yards from her car, gasping for breath, her chest heaving. She watched the car lights come on after the two store employees climbed into their cars.

I'm such an idiot, Reva told herself.

She realized she was still gripping her coat collar with both hands. Staring across the lot as the cars started up, she released her coat and lowered her arms.

"I'm an idiot," she said aloud. "An idiot."

Why did I assume they were chasing me?

Why did I allow myself to become so frightened? I never used to be like that. Never!

"Reva, get a life!" she scolded herself. "I'm losing it. I'm really losing it," she murmured, shaking her head.

She reached into her coat pocket and pulled out

her car key. Her hand trembled as she unlocked the driver's door.

She slid into the leather seat, pulled the door closed, and locked it. Then she tucked her hands into her coat pockets and sat still, very still, staring out into the parking lot, waiting for her breathing to return to normal, waiting for her fear to fade.

I have to stop scaring myself, she thought, watching as a few other store workers crossed the lot and climbed into their cars. I have to stop it—right now.

"I'm Reva Dalby, and I'm not scared of anything," she said out loud. The sound of her voice, smooth and steady, was somehow comforting.

She turned the key in the ignition, clicked on the headlights, and steered the car toward the exit. Division Street was backed up for blocks. Probably an accident.

With an exasperated groan Reva turned off Division onto a side road. I'll go the back way, she told herself. In the rearview mirror she saw the car behind her make the same turn.

Normally, it was only a twenty-minute drive from the store to her home in North Hills, the expensive and exclusive section of Shadyside. Reva knew there was no real reason to hurry. With Michael away in St. Croix, Yvonne, his nanny, had been given the holidays off. So the house would be empty.

But Reva hated to be caught in traffic. It was so frustrating. And she was a girl who didn't like to be frustrated in any way.

She wheeled the little Miata around a corner, sped past a block of small, boxlike houses, then made a sharp turn past a dark, deserted playground.

Lights flashed in her rearview mirror. Glancing up, Reva saw that the car behind her had made the same sharp turn.

The glare of headlights hid the driver from view. But she could see that the car was old and beat-up. A Plymouth, she thought.

"He's not following me," she told herself aloud, pushing her foot down on the gas pedal. The little car shot forward. "Don't start freaking out again, Reva. He's not following you. He's not."

She spun the wheel hard and made a sharp turn onto Park Drive. Houses and trees and hedges whirred by on both sides.

Reva studied the rearview mirror. Twin lights rolled across the back window.

The Plymouth had turned too.

I'm not imagining it. That car *is* following me, Reva realized with a shudder.

But why?

Chapter 5

"GRAB HER BEFORE SHE WAKES UP"

"I followed her," Pres said. "I followed her all the way home. Just to see which way she went. Then I took off."

He held the ketchup bottle over the hamburger and shook it hard. Then he held the bottle still, staring down at the plate as the ketchup puddled onto the meat.

"Like a little hamburger with your ketchup?" Diane asked, shaking her head disapprovingly. She had her white-blond hair tied under a blue and white bandanna, but several strands had frizzed out and fallen over her pale forehead.

"I like a lot of ketchup," Pres muttered, watching

the thick red sauce spread over the bun and onto the plate.

"Should I ask for another bottle?" Diane asked sarcastically. "Or maybe a glass? You could just drink your ketchup."

He didn't reply. Instead, he gestured to the plate of french fries in front of her. "Is that all you're going to eat?"

"Yeah. I'm on a diet." She reached across the Formica table and dipped a fry into the puddle of ketchup on his plate.

"Get your own!" he snapped.

They were sitting across from each other in a dark booth in the back of Freddy's, a small coffee shop in the Old Village of Shadyside. The narrow restaurant smelled of strong coffee and fried onions. Pres and Diane were the only customers.

Pres lifted the hamburger with both hands and took a big bite. Ketchup ran down his chin. He glared across the table at Diane. "Why are you staring at me like that?"

"I'm waiting to hear the rest of your story," she replied, waving a french fry between two fingers but not eating it. "You said you followed her?"

"Yeah. I followed her," he replied, chewing as he talked. "I'm pretty sure she didn't notice me."

"You were careful?"

He nodded, wiping his chin with a paper napkin. "I stayed pretty far back. She didn't see me. I've been following her all week. You know, getting her routine down."

"And?" Diane asked impatiently, dropping the french fry, her gray-blue eyes trained on him.

He swallowed a mouthful of hamburger. "Here's the scoop," he replied, lowering his voice and leaning across the table even though there was no one near. "Dalby leaves the house for work every morning promptly at seven. You can set your watch by him."

"Does Reva go with him?" Diane asked, whispering too.

Pres shook his head, his black hair falling over one eye. He pushed it back off his forehead. "No way. The princess leaves around nine, sometimes a little later. She drives a new car. A little red Miata."

Diane gazed at him thoughtfully. She grabbed a french fry and shoved it into her mouth, chewing rapidly, like a rabbit, not taking her eyes off Pres. "What about servants? Is there a maid? A housekeeper?"

He took a long sip of Coke. "I crept up to the house yesterday morning after Reva left and checked it out. There's no live-in help. A maid arrived about ten minutes after Reva headed off to work. That's all. No one else."

"It can't be that easy," Diane said, trying to tuck her hair under the kerchief.

"Can I have some of your fries?" Pres asked. He grabbed a handful before Diane could reply. "I'm starving tonight."

"Do we have any money to pay for this?" Diane asked, glancing toward the waiter, who was at the front near the door, leaning against the wall, reading a newspaper.

"I've got a few bucks left," Pres told her, patting his back jeans pocket. He reached across the table and squeezed her hand. "In a few days we won't have to worry anymore."

He grinned at her with his Elvis grin. Diane could never resist that sexy grin. She smiled back at him. "As soon as we're rich, I want to go to every movie in town. Ten movies a day! I want to see everything five times!"

He raised a finger to his lips, motioning for her to lower her voice. "There was just one minor problem at Dalby's house," he told her, his grin fading.

"What minor problem?"

"The guard dog," he replied. "A big, ugly monster."

"Huh? Did he go after you when you went up to the house?"

Pres shook his head. "He was on a chain. I think they only unleash him at night."

"Then he's no problem?" Diane asked anxiously.

"Probably no problem," Pres replied.

Diane narrowed her eyes, thinking hard. "Let's go over this carefully," she said, resting her chin in one hand. "After her father leaves at seven, Princess Reva is all alone in the house for two hours."

"Yeah. That's right," Pres said, greedily finishing off her french fries. "She must be asleep until at least eight-thirty. She doesn't open her bedroom blinds until then. And there's no one else there."

"So the best time to grab her is at her house

before she wakes up," Diane said, thinking out loud.

"Yeah," Pres quickly agreed. "Piece of cake."

"Then let's kidnap her tomorrow morning," Diane said, an eager smile spreading across her face.

Chapter 6

DOWN, BOY!

The windshield and windows were clouded over with thick white mist. Pale light filtered in from the full moon above.

Outside the small car, the air hung cold and still. The bare tree branches clung together as if trying to keep warm.

Victor had turned off the engine after parking on the cliff edge. For a while, before they started to kiss, they had stared out through the windshield, gazing down at the town of Shadyside spread out below.

River Ridge, the tall rock cliff overlooking the Conononka River, was a popular parking spot for Shadyside High students. But on this frosty night Victor's car was the only one there.

Staring out at the star-dotted sky, Victor huddled

in his down jacket and wondered if this was really happening.

As the windshield started to fog up, she leaned over, wrapped her hands—warm hands—around his neck, pulled him to her, and started to kiss him.

She moved her mouth against his, tiny sighs escaping her lips. Her warm hands, surprisingly strong, held him tightly, pressing his face to hers.

The kiss lasted a long time.

When he finally ended it, reaching up to pull her hands from the back of his neck, Victor was breathing hard. His face felt hot. His heart pounded.

She smiled at him, a devilish smile, then lowered her forehead to the shoulder of his coat.

"We—we shouldn't be up here," Victor stammered.

She giggled and brushed his hot cheek with her lips.

"No. Really," he insisted, his voice sounding tight and shrill in the heavy air in the small car. "We—we shouldn't. I mean—"

Reva squeezed his hand. "It's okay," she whispered, her blue eyes glowing in the pale moonlight that filtered through the windshield.

"But it isn't right," Victor insisted, turning to face her. "Pam and I—we're serious about each other. We—"

Reva snickered. "You *are* a serious guy, aren't you?" she said teasingly.

"When you called me tonight, I—I didn't know. I mean—" Victor struggled for words.

Reva didn't give him a chance to protest. She

reached up and pulled his head down to her again. Then she pressed her lips against his, hard, harder.

She kissed him until she could barely breathe.

He's so good-looking, she thought.

I had to call him. I couldn't resist.

She let her coppery hair fall over his face and kissed him again.

Reva chuckled to herself. She wondered what her cousin Pam was doing right then. Waiting by the phone for Victor to call?

Pam is such a loser, Reva thought scornfully.

Victor is just too good-looking for a loser like Pam.

Diane gripped the steering wheel tightly in both cold hands. The heater still wasn't working. She glared at Pres. "Will you stop cracking your knuckles?" she demanded shrilly. "I thought you said you weren't nervous."

Pres gave the knuckles one more loud pop, then lowered his hands to his lap. "I'm n-not nervous. I'm a little excited. I never kidnapped anyone before, you know."

"Neither have I," Diane replied sharply. "So stop trying to drive me crazy. First you wouldn't stop tapping your foot. Now you're cracking your knuckles till I'm ready to scream."

Pres turned his gaze to the Dalby house at the top of the sloping lawn. "Sorry," he muttered. "Look. There goes Dalby."

Pres's beat-up Plymouth was parked at the curb three houses down, the engine running. From there,

Pres and Diane could see a corner of the Dalbys' big stone house and the three-car garage beside it.

A silver Mercedes pulled out of the drive between two tall hedges, stopped at the street, then headed to the right, away from where Pres and Diane watched.

"It's not bright enough," Diane complained. "I can't really see him."

"It's him," Pres said in a whisper, his eyes trained on the Mercedes until it disappeared down the tree-lined block. "There goes Mr. King-of-the-World Dalby."

"Leaving his princess all alone," Diane said. She shifted into Drive. "Shall we get going?"

Pres put a hand over hers to stop her. "No. Wait. Let's wait t-ten minutes. Make sure Dalby doesn't come back."

Diane obediently shifted back into Park. She sighed impatiently. "What time is it?"

Pres glanced at the dashboard clock, then remembered it was stuck at three-thirty. "Must be a little after seven. I told you, Dalby leaves at seven. I watched four mornings in a row. He's always right on schedule."

He started to crack his knuckles. Remembering Diane's protests, he stopped himself. A car rolled by, a station wagon loaded with kids. Pres ducked low in the passenger seat and turned his face away.

"Oh, sigh," Diane murmured. "I wish this was over."

"And we were home counting our money," Pres added, tapping his fingers on the knees of his jeans.

"Where's her bedroom—upstairs or down?" Diane asked, her tight voice revealing her nervousness.

"Upstairs. On the left," Pres answered. "I watched the light go on two different nights. I know how to find it."

Diane tugged at a strand of hair that tumbled out from a black baseball cap pulled low over her forehead. Her worried expression suddenly changed. She flashed Pres a toothy smile. "This really is like the movies—isn't it!" she exclaimed.

Pres didn't smile back. He narrowed his dark eyes. "Yeah. But I don't exactly feel like a movie star," he said dryly.

"You will when we have a million dollars!" Diane insisted.

"Let's get it over with," he said. "Come on. Pull up." He motioned with both hands.

Diane shifted into Drive and inched the car along the curb until they were at the Dalbys' driveway. "Should I pull up the drive?" she asked, peering at the tall hedges that surrounded the Dalby property on all sides.

"No. Keep it here," Pres instructed. "By the drive. But don't block the drive. It might look suspicious."

He grabbed the door handle. "And keep the engine going. Once we've got her, we have to bomb out of here—fast."

He started to push open the passenger door.

"Hey—kiss for luck!" Diane called after him.

He leaned toward her and accepted a quick kiss. Then he jumped out of the car and hurried toward the driveway, his head low, his hands buried in his jacket pockets.

The morning sun was a red ball climbing up the Dalbys' enormous house. Pres's breath came out in puffs of white steam as he jogged toward the side of the house, keeping in the deep shadow of the tall hedge.

He was halfway up the drive when he saw the black Doberman attack dog coming for him.

Pres stopped short. "Hey—where's your chain?" he called.

The big dog lowered its head and snarled out a warning. Its eyes flashed red and locked on Pres. It pulled back its lips and, with another furious snarl, bared its teeth.

Pres fought back the wave of fear that surged over him.

"I'm ready f-for you, doggie," he called. His hand was trembling as he reached into his jacket pocket.

He kept his eyes on the growling dog. The dog stopped at the edge of the driveway, preparing to attack.

Pres pulled out the strips of bacon he had brought, and thrust out his hand to show the dog. "Bacon!" he cried. "No dog can resist bacon—right?"

Pres tossed the bacon onto the grass.

"Go get it, boy. See? Pres is your friend."

The dog ignored the bacon. Opening its jaw and pulling back its lip to bare its teeth, the Doberman leapt for Pres's throat.

Chapter 7

A PIECE OF CAKE

Pres cried out as the snarling dog attacked. He thrust up both arms to shield himself.

The weight of the big Doberman forced Pres to stagger back into the hedge. The dog's mouth closed around the sleeve of Pres's leather bomber jacket and held on.

Pres frantically reached with his free hand into his jacket pocket. Struggling to shake his jacket sleeve free from the dog's grasp, he pulled out a chloroform-soaked handkerchief.

Wrenching his arm free, he grabbed the dog's snout.

"Yaaaii!" Pres cried out as the dog nipped his hand.

The Doberman snapped its jaws, pulled back its

head, then let out a snarl of rage as it struggled to squirm free.

But Pres held on to the dog, wrapping his hand around its snout, holding its mouth shut as he pressed the chloroformed handkerchief over the dog's nostrils.

The dog's chest heaved. Its head snapped back as it struggled to breathe.

Got to hold on! Got to hold on! Pres told himself.

The animal's eyes glared angrily at Pres. Its head twisted one way, then the other.

Then the eyes closed. The struggle ended. The dog slumped heavily to the ground with a long groan.

Pres stepped back. Swallowing hard, he stared down at the dog. It lay stretched out on its side, its jaws open wide, breathing steadily, quietly.

Pres stuffed the chloroformed cloth back into his pocket and zipped the pocket shut. Always be prepared, he thought. That's my motto.

He stood in the shade of the hedge for a moment, observing the unconscious dog, waiting for his own breathing to return to normal.

He touched the back pocket of his jeans, made sure the small pistol was still there. He could have used it on the dog, he knew. It would have been quicker, easier.

But noisy.

A pistol shot might have awakened Princess Reva, sleeping upstairs. And Pres didn't want that. He wanted to save that pleasure for himself.

Feeling a little better, his blood still pumping at

his temples, Pres examined the sleeve of his bomber jacket. Just a slight scratch. No big deal.

With a last glance at the defeated guard dog, he quickly made his way around the side of the house to the back door. Two of the three garage doors were open. He could see Reva's red Miata parked inside.

Nice car, he thought, stopping at the back stoop to admire it for a moment. Maybe I'll get one of those with the ransom money.

He snickered to himself. Maybe I'll get *two!*

"First things first," he muttered to himself. He pulled the small silver pistol from his back pocket. Stepping up to the back door, he tapped the gun grip a few times against the pane of glass closest to the doorknob.

The rising sun reflected in the window glass. The kitchen on the other side of the door lay mostly hidden in long shadows.

"Easy does it," Pres murmured. He tapped the gun handle a few times more, testing the glass, testing his touch.

He tapped harder. Harder.

He gave the windowpane a hard hit. The glass cracked, then shattered, dropping onto the kitchen floor.

Pres reached in the window, fumbled around till he found the lock, and turned it. A second later he was standing in the kitchen.

"Wow," he whispered to himself, glancing quickly around. The kitchen was bigger than his entire apartment. Bigger than some houses he'd been in.

Look at that, he marveled. *Two* refrigerators! How much can people eat?

He forced himself to stop sight-seeing. Taking a deep breath, the pistol still clenched in his hand, he made his way to the front hall.

The dark carpet was thick and plush. His sneakers sank into it. His footsteps were silent.

The hall stretched on endlessly. Big oil paintings covered the walls on both sides. Pres glanced into the living room. Still filled with the same delicate antique furniture.

He paused at the bottom of the carpeted stairway, leaning against the smooth polished-wood banister. He listened.

Silence. Beautiful silence.

He was all alone. All alone in Dalbyland.

Just me and Reva, he thought, gazing up the steep stairway.

This is going to be a piece of cake. Piece of cake.

Holding the pistol at his waist, he started up the stairs to Reva's room.

Chapter 8

SIRENS

"Where *is* he?" Diane asked herself, leaning over the steering wheel, trying to see up to the Dalbys' house.

"What's taking Pres so long?"

She had the engine running and the heater on full blast even though it didn't do any good. Diane still felt cold all over. Her throat ached, suddenly dry as cotton.

"Pres—where *are* you?"

Pres had instructed her not to move. But she decided she had to have a better view. She shoved the gearshift into Drive and inched the car forward until she could see up the long driveway.

No sign of him.

Hurry. Hurry, Pres.

What was that dark lump by the side of the driveway?

At first Diane thought it was some kind of black plastic garbage bag. Squinting through the passenger window, she saw it was a dog.

Pres must have had to use the chloroform, she realized.

Diane was still staring at the unmoving dog when she heard the sirens.

Her hand trembling, she rolled down the window to hear better.

The sirens were a faint wail on the still air. Far away, Diane realized. She held her breath, listening hard. The sirens were getting louder.

Closer.

Police sirens.

They're coming here. To the Dalbys' house, Diane told herself.

Pres must have tripped some kind of burglar alarm.

A chill of fear made Diane shudder. She rolled up the window, but the sour wail of the sirens lingered in her ears.

She gazed up the long drive to the house. The red sun was up to the roof now, the house bathed in early morning light.

"Pres—where are you? Pres—please get *out* of there!"

The sirens grew louder.

Diane's panic began to constrict her breathing. Pres had been inside for only a few minutes, but she was losing all sense of time.

She pressed down on the gas pedal, and the engine responded with a roar. She shifted into Drive.

Pres, I don't want to leave you here, she thought, staring frantically at the house. I don't want to leave you here. But if the police are coming, I have no choice.

She squeezed the wheel in her icy hands.

"If the police come, I'm *out* of here!" she cried aloud.

She leaned against the wheel, every muscle in her body tensed, listening, listening as the sirens droned closer.

Pres crept along the endless upstairs hall, his sneakers sinking into the thick white carpet. Yellow morning sunlight poured in from a skylight overhead.

So many rooms, Pres thought, shaking his head. He'd never been up here.

He peeked into an open doorway. A king-size bed, unmade, a satiny quilt half on the floor, silky sheets crumpled over it, stood on a diagonal in the center of the room. Dark bookshelves lined one wall from floor to ceiling. A low, sleek dresser stood against the opposite wall with an enormous mirror above it. A wide-screen TV was perched on a cabinet across from the bed.

This must be the master bedroom, Pres realized. He couldn't resist spying. He took a cautious step into the room, his eyes darting around, taking in everything.

Beyond the bedroom the light had been left on in

an enormous bathroom. Through the bathroom doorway Pres could see a Jacuzzi.

I'll get one of those when I'm a millionaire, he thought.

I'll have a big house like this one, with a hundred rooms with carpet as soft as a featherbed.

And I'll buy a pinball machine. Two pinball machines. No—a whole room full of pinball machines.

He backed out of Robert Dalby's bedroom, suddenly remembering his mission.

First, I have to get Reva.

Her bedroom had to be the next one down on the other side of the hall.

The door was closed.

Silently, his heart beginning to pound, Pres made his way across the hall. His shadow, cast by the skylight overhead, fell over Reva's door.

Pres took a deep breath. Then, raising the pistol, he turned the knob and pushed open Reva's bedroom door.

"Good morning!" he called.

Chapter 9

A FEW SMALL PROBLEMS

Diane was so frightened, she felt like screaming.

Her impulse was to honk the horn, to signal Pres that he had to get out of there.

"What's keeping him? What's keeping him?"

Couldn't he find Reva's room? He claimed he had scoped it out, that he knew where it was.

He claimed this was going to be a breeze. No big deal.

So where *was* he?

Was Reva giving him trouble? Did he run into someone else in the house? Had they captured him? Knocked him unconscious? Tied him up? Called the police?

What? What? What?

A million questions roared through her head. But they were being drowned out by the shrill sirens.

Closer. Closer.

It's the police, Diane knew. And they're only a few blocks away.

Pres set off an alarm. I've got to get out of here. But how can I leave him?

She rolled down the window, the sound of the sirens growing even louder. She stuck her head out and stared up the driveway.

Pres—please hurry! Please!

We're going to be caught.

Can't you hear the sirens? We're going to be caught!

"Good m-morning!" Pres stammered in a high, tight voice he didn't recognize.

He stepped into Reva's bedroom.

And stared at the bed.

The empty bed.

The pillow lay on the floor. The blankets had been tossed in a heap on the floor. White- and red-striped pajamas were balled up in a corner of the bed.

Pres took in the empty room, his mouth hanging open. Stunned, he froze, still as a statue.

He stared hard, as if staring would make her appear.

As if he were only imagining that the bedroom was empty.

"Hey—" The sound of his own voice snapped him back to reality. "Hey—"

Then he heard the sirens.

The bedroom window was open just a crack. The flimsy white curtains fluttered gently. The rise and fall of the shrill sirens floated in through the window.

Sirens?

So close?

"Oh, wow!" Pres uttered.

He realized instantly what had happened. He must have set off a silent burglar alarm when he broke the window in back. A burglar alarm hooked up to the Shadyside police.

Now they were on their way. Almost here, judging by the sirens.

And there he stood, staring at an empty, unmade bed.

"Aaaagh!" A roar of anger and frustration burst from his chest.

"Reva—where are you?" he screamed.

Then, gaining control, he turned and ran from the room.

Into the long, sunny hall, his sneakers padding over the thick white carpet, his shadow fleeing just ahead of him.

Past Dalby's luxurious bedroom.

To the shiny-banistered stairway.

Reva—where are you? Where did you go?

How did you escape?

How did you mess up my plans?

Down the stairs, two at a time, leaning on the sleek banister, the pistol still in his hand.

The front hallway a blur of green and brown. The front door his only obstacle to escape.

Pres fumbled with the chain. The sirens sounded as if they were right outside. In the driveway?

No. Please—no.

He turned the lock. He pulled open the heavy oak door.

Outside now, he ran down the driveway. Ran past the still-unconscious dog. Ran so fast his chest felt about to burst.

"Diane!" He called her name as he pulled open the passenger door and dived into the seat. The sirens were so loud now, so loud and close. Just around the corner.

"Diane—go!"

"But—but—Reva—?" She gaped at him, her features twisted in confusion.

"Just drive!" he screamed. *"Go!"*

"Okay, Pres!"

Diane grabbed the wheel with both hands, leaned forward, stepped on the gas—and the car stalled out.

Chapter 10

THE POLICE MOVE IN

"Go! Go! Go!" Pres screamed, pounding frantically on the dashboard.

"I can't! It—stalled!" Diane's hand trembled as she turned the key. The engine made a sick, grinding sound.

The wail of the sirens grew louder, so loud they seemed to be coming from inside the car.

Diane turned the key again, pumping the gas pedal.

Pres turned his head to stare out the back window. The sirens were loud. He knew the police would be turning the corner any second.

"We're trapped here! Sitting ducks!"

The old car wheezed, coughed—and the engine sputtered to life.

"Yes!" Diane cried happily. She stomped hard

on the gas pedal and the car shot forward. "Yes! Yes!"

Pres kept his head turned to the back window, his dark eyes narrowed, his face knotted in fear. The shrieking sirens seemed to surround them.

Diane pulled the wheel hard to the left, and the car squealed around a corner. She floored the gas pedal, gripping the wheel tightly with both hands, leaning forward as if trying to get as far away as possible.

Another squealing turn. Then another.

The sirens faded to a distant howl.

Pres let out a long sigh and turned back to face the windshield. "We got away," he murmured breathlessly. He sank low in the seat, raising his knees to the dashboard. "We got away."

"That was close," Diane said, her eyes on the road, her hands still gripping the wheel tightly.

"Yeah." Pres uttered a nervous giggle. "Real close."

A smile slowly formed on Diane's face as the tension fell away. "Kind of exciting," she said quietly.

"Reva wasn't there," Pres told her, scowling.

"Huh? You mean you couldn't find her?"

"No. She wasn't there," he snapped. "Her room was empty."

Diane's smile faded. "Don't worry, honey." She reached out and patted Pres's hand. "We'll get her next time. She won't get away."

Reva tapped her long fingernails on the glass counter, gazing at the glass doors across the aisle, watching the morning shoppers file into the store. She yawned and turned to Francine, who was busily arranging sample perfume bottles on the countertop.

"Reva, I want to show you something," Francine said, bending down to slide open a door to the floor cabinets.

Why don't you get your nose done, Francine? Reva thought with a sneer. Then maybe you could talk through your mouth and people could understand you.

"I like what you've done to your hair," Reva told her.

"What?" Francine glanced up fretfully from the cabinet. "Oh. I was late this morning. I didn't have time to wash it."

Why bother? Reva thought nastily.

Francine stood up and straightened her blouse. She carried a small white plastic case over to Reva and unzipped it. "We have a special gift today," she said, opening the case and holding it up for Reva to inspect.

Thrills, Reva thought sarcastically. Can I stand the excitement?

"If they buy the two-ounce perfume," Francine said, pointing to a shimmering gold bottle on the counter, "they get this little kit. See? It has a cologne, a bath gel, and a spray deodorant."

Francine lifted each little bottle out of the leather case as she showed it to Reva. As she raised the deodorant, she accidentally sprayed a little of it into the air.

"Yuck!" Reva cried, making a disgusted face. "It smells like bug spray!"

"Shhhh!" Francine raised a finger to her lips and glanced around quickly, seeing if anyone had overheard. "It's a nice gift."

"Is that a new lipstick you're wearing?" Reva asked her.

"I'm not wearing any lipstick," Francine replied, unaware that Reva had asked her question to be cruel.

So *that's* why you look like you died three weeks ago! Reva thought.

Francine handed the gift pack to Reva and hurried to the far end of the perfume counter to help a customer. Reva sighed and leaned against the glass counter, daydreaming about Victor and the night before.

She pictured the steamed-up car windows, the chill night air, the soft darkness all around. She thought about kissing Victor, holding on to him, holding him to her. He was so solid, so good-looking.

A slender, blond-haired woman moving quickly down the counter interrupted Reva's thoughts. Reva recognized her.

It's the woman in the tacky fake-fur jacket, Reva thought. She comes by every morning and pretends she's going to buy something. But she's only interested in spraying herself with perfume for free.

"Is that jacket real chipmunk or imitation?" Reva asked as the woman picked up a large bottle of cologne from the counter.

"I beg your pardon?" The woman set down the bottle and eyed Reva suspiciously.

"I was just admiring your jacket," Reva said, putting on her phoniest smile. "Can I help you with anything?"

The woman tossed her hair behind her shoulder with one hand. "Yes. I'm looking for something a little different," she said, studying the sample bottles. "Something a little tart. Not so sweet."

Reva grinned at her. "I have something new you might like. It's not too sweet." She pulled the small bottle of spray deodorant from the gift case, covering the label with her hand. "Here."

The woman held up the back of her hand, and Reva sprayed a mist of deodorant onto it. The woman rubbed it into her hand, then sniffed it. "Mmmmm. Very good. It *is* different. Could I have a little bit more?"

Reva obliged. She sprayed more deodorant onto the woman's hand. The woman rubbed it on her neck and behind her ears. "What is it called?"

"Arrid Extra Dry," Reva muttered.

"What?" The woman leaned forward to hear better.

"Arid Nights," Reva said. "It's French. It's two hundred dollars an ounce."

"I'll definitely come back later and buy a bottle," the woman said. Sniffing her hand, she hurried away.

Reva watched the back of the red fake-fur jacket until it disappeared around a corner. Then she laughed out loud. This isn't such a boring job after all, she thought.

Francine, busy with three customers at once, had her back turned. Reva decided to take advantage of that fact. She ducked out of the counter and escaped, losing herself in the crowd.

She wandered along the aisles of the main floor, heading toward the back. Spotting her cousin Pam in the stationery department, she hurried over to say hello.

Pam wore a bright green sweater over brown slacks. Her blond hair was pulled straight back in a ponytail, held in place with a silky green ribbon. As usual, Reva noted, she wore no makeup, not even lipstick.

She's always so fresh looking, Reva thought with scorn. She could do Ivory soap commercials.

"Reva, I saw you come in this morning," Pam said. "You were so early."

"Yeah. I came in early with my dad," Reva told her. "He left me a note last night that he wanted to talk, so—"

"You were out last night?" Pam asked.

Yeah. With *your* boyfriend, fresh face, Reva thought.

"Maybe," Reva replied coyly. She gave Pam a teasing grin.

"New boyfriend?" Pam asked.

I love Pam's childlike innocence, Reva thought sarcastically. It's so *cute!*

"Just a friend," Reva replied, deliberately sounding mysterious.

"I'm going out with Victor tonight," Pam revealed, her green eyes lighting up.

"That's nice," Reva replied casually. "He seems like an okay guy."

He kisses okay. *Real* okay, Reva thought.

"I can't stop thinking about him," Pam gushed. She leaned close to Reva so she wouldn't be overheard by anyone else. "I think this may be the real thing," Pam whispered. "I mean, I think I'm really in love!"

"That's great," Reva replied without enthusiasm. "That's really great, Pam."

Why can't Pam be smart for once and find a *rich* boyfriend? Reva thought. Victor doesn't have a dime, and neither does she.

"I'd like you to get to know Victor," Pam continued, smiling eagerly at her cousin. "I think you'll really like him."

I'm trying, Reva thought, struggling not to laugh in Pam's face. I'm trying, Pam.

"Have fun tonight," Reva said. "I'm glad *someone* is having an exciting life."

Pam placed a hand on Reva's shoulder and felt the soft silky fabric of her blouse. "It's holiday time, Reva. I'm sure your life will get more exciting real soon."

"Why are we doing this?" Diane demanded, turning into North Hills. The evening sky was dark. She switched on the high beams.

"I told you," Pres said edgily. "Sometimes Reva gets home from the store before her father. Sometimes she's all alone in the house in the evening. Maybe we can drop in and surprise her."

Pres had been brooding all day about their failed

kidnapping attempt. He had paced back and forth in his small living room, muttering to himself, shaking his head, until Diane couldn't take it anymore. With an angry cry she had fled the apartment and gone for a long walk.

She returned a little after sunset to find Pres waiting for her, eager to drive back to Shadyside, back to the Dalbys' house.

"Reva will be alone. We can do it now. I know we can," Pres urged with growing enthusiasm.

But as Diane turned the Plymouth into Reva's block and the big stone house came into view, she quickly saw that Reva was *not* alone.

"Cops!" she cried, and jammed her foot down hard on the brake.

She and Pres stared into the darkness. There were three black and white squad cars parked at the curb and one in the Dalbys' driveway. Two officers with bright halogen flashlights were pacing the front lawn, their lights sweeping the ground.

"I don't believe it!" Pres declared. "Don't stop! Keep going!"

Diane eased her foot off the brake. "I guess they're searching for clues."

"Rich people," Pres muttered bitterly, ignoring her. "Here it is night, and the cops are still here from this morning. You think they'd work this hard for some average family?"

"Let's just get away," Diane said with a shudder.

She pressed down on the gas and started to ease the car past the Dalby house.

But a bright glare of white light in the windshield made her slam on the brakes. "Hey—!" she cried out as two dark-uniformed police officers loomed over the car. Their lights beamed onto her startled face from the side windows.

"Pull it over," one of them mouthed through the closed window, his eyes narrowed, his features set in a hard scowl.

"They—they've caught us," Pres stammered.

Chapter 11

"HE'LL GET US ALL KILLED"

"Wh-what should I do?" Diane uttered, her eyes wide with fear.

"Pull over," Pres told her. "We can't get away. A neighbor must have seen the car this morning. We're caught. Caught!"

Diane obediently pulled the car to the curb and shoved the gearshift into Park. "In the movies we'd make a run for it," she muttered.

"This isn't the movies," Pres replied bitterly.

The police officer tapped hard on the window with his flashlight. Diane lowered the window. "Yes, officer?" she called out in a tiny voice.

The man bent over, peering in at the two occupants, his face expressionless, his eyes narrowed.

"You've got a headlight out," he said finally. "The left one. See?" He pointed with his flashlight.

Diane wanted to laugh out loud. Somehow she remained silent. "I didn't know," she said in her meek little voice. "It must have just happened."

"I could give you a ticket," the officer said, turning his gaze on Pres. "But I'm kind of busy here. Why don't you just go get it fixed?"

"Oh, thanks, officer," Diane replied gratefully. "Thanks a lot."

She started to roll up the window, but stopped when Pres called out, "What's going on here? Why all the black-and-whites?"

"Nothing that concerns you," the man replied sharply. He turned and headed back up to the Dalbys' front lawn, taking long strides.

Diane made sure the window was closed before she burst out laughing. "Nothing that concerns you," she repeated, grinning at Pres.

Pres didn't share her mirth. "Let's get out of here," he snapped, his eyes on the police officers combing the front lawn. He slumped low in the seat, a scowl on his face.

Diane eased the car away from the curb, turned at the first corner, and headed back toward Pres's apartment in Waynesbridge. Pres remained silent for most of the ride, thinking hard, his eyes fixed straight ahead on the dark, winding road.

"There's no way we can get Reva at her house now," he said finally. "Not with all those cops around."

"You mean you're giving up?" Diane cried, disappointed.

"No way," Pres murmured. "I have a new plan."

"All right!" Diane's expression brightened. She pulled into a McDonald's. "You hungry?" She had to ask three times. Pres was lost in thought.

A few minutes later, tucked in a booth in the back of the restaurant, Pres leaned over the table and revealed his plan in a low voice. "We'll take Reva from the department store," he said.

Diane wiped a smear of ketchup off her cheek with a napkin. "How?"

"She works at a perfume counter, see," Pres told her, his eyes darting nervously around the brightly lit restaurant, making sure no one could hear. "I checked it out the other morning."

"She didn't see you—did she?" Diane interrupted.

"No way. The store was crowded. I watched her from another aisle. Her perfume counter is right across from a side door that opens onto the street."

Diane swallowed a mouthful of cheeseburger. "So we park on the street, run in, grab her, and pull her out?"

Pres shook his head. "No. We create some kind of distraction. We get Reva to step out from behind the counter. Then she's only a few feet from the door. If she's out in the aisle, it'll be easy to drag her outside without anyone seeing. Especially if we do it first thing in the morning. There aren't many customers when the store first opens. And Reva has the first shift before that other saleswoman arrives."

Diane took a long sip of her Coke, her eyes on Pres, thinking hard.

"Why are you staring at me?" he demanded edgily. "It's a good plan. It'll work."

She set down the paper cup. "Yeah. Probably," she replied. "But we need Danny."

Pres reacted with surprise. "Huh? My brother?"

Diane nodded. She crinkled the paper cheeseburger wrapper into a ball. "Yeah. We're going to need Danny."

"What for?" Pres demanded. "I can pull Reva out the door. I don't need Danny for that."

"We need him to drive," she said. "If you're going to pull Reva out the door, I have to create the distraction. I have to get her to come out from behind the counter, right? So we need Danny to drive."

Pres scowled. "I don't like it. You know Danny. You know how he loses his cool."

"We need him," Diane insisted.

"Danny and his headaches," Pres muttered. "He's so hot-tempered, Diane. You know my older brother. When he gets excited, he's totally out of control. If something goes wrong, he could get us all killed!"

"Shhhhh." Diane spread her hand over Pres's mouth. "Danny'll stay in the car. That's all. We need him to drive once we've got Reva. No problem."

"Well . . ." Pres shook his head, still scowling.

"Come on, Pres," Diane pleaded. "Call Danny as soon as we get home, okay?"

Pres climbed to his feet. "Let's go." He headed for the door.

"Will you do it?" Diane hurried to catch up.

"Yeah. I guess," he replied, pushing open the door to the parking lot. "When do you want to grab Reva?"

"It's almost Christmas. There's lots of things I want to buy with that ransom money," Diane said, taking his arm. "Let's do it tomorrow morning."

Chapter 12

COUNTER ATTACK

Reva pulled the corn muffin and coffee container from the brown paper bag and set them on the counter. She tore off a chunk of the muffin and took a dainty bite, brushing crumbs off the glass with her long fingernails.

"Reva—what are you doing?" Francine stepped up beside her, an angry expression on her face.

"Eating a muffin," Reva replied coolly. She held up a crumbly chunk. "Want a bite?"

"But you're twenty-five minutes late!" Francine cried shrilly, pointing to the clock above the doorway. "You know you were supposed to be at the counter first thing this morning. It's a good thing I came in early today. I had to cover for you."

Reva concentrated on pulling the lid off the

coffee container. "I know. I couldn't decide which sweater to wear." She turned to Francine to better show off her pale blue sweater. "Do you like this one? It's cashmere."

"I just wiped off the counter," Francine complained. "You're getting crumbs all over it."

"It's a very crumbly muffin," Reva replied with a full mouth. "It's pretty good though. Sure you don't want a little? Oh. I forgot. You're on a diet."

Reva chuckled to herself, watching crumbs fall onto the glass counter. She took a sip of coffee, the hot liquid burning her tongue, then set down the container in a round brown puddle. "I think this cup is leaking. What a mess."

Francine let out an angry cry. "I'm going to make a phone call," she said through clenched teeth. "You'd better get this cleaned up before Ms. Smith sees it."

"Yeah. Sure thing," Reva replied under her breath. She watched Francine storm off toward the employees' lounge. "What's *her* problem anyway?"

Reva raised the last piece of corn muffin to her mouth. Then she studied herself in the mirror, adjusting the floppy navy blue hat she had pulled over her hair.

The hat was the real reason Reva had been late. She just couldn't get it to sit right. It had taken nearly half an hour. She planned "accidentally" to run into Victor later, and she hoped he liked it.

Gazing down the aisle, she saw two people approaching slowly. A boy and a girl. They appeared to be seventeen or eighteen.

The boy was tall and dark and carried a raincoat over one arm. The girl was shorter, shabbily dressed, kind of plain, very thin.

What a bleach job, Reva thought scornfully, staring at the girl's hair. Didn't anyone tell her you have to do the roots too?

Reva picked up her coffee and turned away. I hope those two losers don't come over here, she thought. I'll just tell them ankle bracelets are in the basement. Or maybe I'll suggest they exchange tattoos for Christmas.

She chuckled. I'm so nasty, she thought, feeling very pleased with herself.

She found herself thinking about Victor again. She had called him late the night before. He had promised to break a date with Pam and see her instead.

I know I'm going to hate myself for this, Reva thought, smiling. But it's kind of fun while it lasts. . . .

It's so boring around here. I need a challenge.

Like Victor.

She glanced up to see the two tacky teenagers approaching her. Why don't they go shoplift in some other department? she thought coldly.

Suddenly the blond girl dived to the floor. The dark-haired boy jumped back, a startled expression on his face.

Reva turned around, pretending not to be aware of them.

"My contact!" the girl cried from down on the floor. "I dropped my contact lens!"

Reva took a long sip of coffee.

"Help me. I can't see a thing!" the girl cried shrilly.

Leaning on the counter, Reva glanced down. The girl was on her hands and knees, running a hand over the black and white squares of tile.

The boy suddenly stepped up in front of her, his raincoat still draped over one arm. He's kind of good-looking, Reva thought. I like those dark, smoldering eyes.

"Can somebody help me?" the girl called from the floor. She had crawled between the perfume counter and the side door to the store. "I can't see a thing."

Reva, pretending not to hear, lowered her head, trying to hide under the floppy hat. She busied herself straightening the sleeves of her cashmere sweater.

"Can you help us?" the boy asked. "I don't have my glasses with me. I'm as blind as she is."

Reva took another sip of coffee before answering. "Sorry. I'm on my break."

"I can't find it!" the girl called.

"Couldn't you come out and help us?" the boy pleaded. "It'll only take a second."

Reva set down the cup. "Sorry. I'm not allowed to leave my post."

To Reva's surprise, the boy uttered an angry curse.

"Hey—!" she shouted as he grabbed her arm with both hands and started to pull her through the cosmetics counter's swinging door and toward the exit.

Chapter 13

"LET'S JUST KILL HER"

"Let go of me!" Reva cried angrily.

Ignoring her protests, the boy continued to pull her toward the door. "It'll t-take only a second," he repeated. His eyes, Reva saw, were wide with anger—and fear.

"Let go!" She struggled to pull free.

"What's going on here?" an angry voice demanded.

The boy let go.

Reva turned to see Ms. Smith glaring at her. "Reva, what are you doing?"

"M-me?" Reva sputtered.

"I found it!" the blond girl cried from the floor. She climbed quickly to her feet. "I dropped my contact, that's all," she told Ms. Smith.

She and the boy hurried out the side door without looking back.

Reva rubbed the sleeve of her sweater. "Weird," she muttered. Like it's *my* job to find her stupid contact, she thought angrily. What jerks!

"Reva, you were very late this morning," Ms. Smith scolded, eyeing the yellow muffin crumbs and brown coffee circle on the glass countertop.

"Yes. My father asked me to take his new Mercedes to the garage," Reva replied, casually putting Ms. Smith in her place.

"Let's just kill her!" Pres's brother Danny cried, turning the wheel hard, his brown workboot pressed hard on the gas pedal. "Why don't we kill her?"

The old Plymouth sputtered, then shot forward. Danny leaned over the wheel, his dark eyes narrowed angrily. He looked like an older, flabbier version of Pres. He had the same dark hair and soulful eyes. But his face was round with puffy cheeks. And even though he was only twenty-five, he had a big belly that bulged under his gray sweatshirt.

Pres was tense in the passenger seat beside his brother, his eyes on the road ahead. Diane sat on the right-hand side in the backseat, nervously toying with her hair.

"We won't get any money if we just kill her," she called up to Danny. "What's the point of killing her?"

"Well, she's messed you up twice, hasn't she?" Danny replied. "So why not just kill her?"

"Shut up and drive," Pres snapped bitterly. "You just joined us this morning, and already you want to kill her."

"The whole point is to kidnap Reva and get her father to pay," Diane explained patiently. "There's no point in killing her."

"Danny talks big," Pres muttered. "He isn't about to kill anyone."

Danny chuckled. He took his eyes off the road and turned to Pres. "Hey, man, don't get on my case. I'm not the one who goofed up twice."

Pres scowled and turned his face toward the window.

They drove on in silence for a while, past bare wintry-looking fields and farmhouses with chimneys sending up clouds of white smoke into the gray morning sky.

"Big-time criminals," Danny scoffed, shaking his head. He gave his brother a hard shove on the shoulder of his bomber jacket. "You're going to steal the girl? You couldn't steal second base in a Little League game!" Danny tossed back his head, laughing as if he had made the cleverest joke ever told, and nearly crashed the car into a truck parked on the shoulder of the highway.

"Watch where you're going!" Diane screamed.

Danny swerved just in time.

"I told you he'd get us killed," Pres muttered.

"My kid brother is a big-time criminal." Danny chuckled.

"Let's calm down and try to get it together," Diane urged. "I mean, come on. Both of you. Lay off each other, okay?"

"Hey, I'm not the one who messed up!" Danny cried, suddenly angry. "I'm just the driver—remember?"

"Then just drive," Pres muttered. "And shut your face."

"I can't believe I gave up a day of work for this," Danny grumbled, ignoring Pres. "Five thousand dollars you promised me. What a joke."

"We can still get the money," Diane interrupted from the back. She leaned forward, putting both hands on the back of Pres's seat. "We can still grab Reva, you know."

"How?" Pres asked skeptically, turning to face her. "She's seen us. She's seen both of us. How are we going to get near her?"

"She hasn't seen Danny," Diane replied.

Pres rolled his eyes.

"So now I'm doing all the work?" Danny complained. He roared through a red light.

"Shut up and let her talk," Pres snapped impatiently. "You have an idea, Diane?"

She nodded. "What about the stockroom at the store, Pres? You said Reva works in the stockroom every afternoon, right?"

"Yeah. From three to five," Pres replied.

"That was Pres's old hangout," Danny said, smirking. "Till he got caught with some goodies under his coat." He uttered a high-pitched giggle. "Big-time criminal!" he scoffed, shaking his head.

"Danny, give Pres a break," Diane pleaded. She squeezed Pres's shoulder. "So can we hide in the stockroom? Can we drag Reva out of there?"

Pres thought about it. "Yeah. Probably," he

replied without enthusiasm. "There are a lot of cartons and shelves and stuff to hide behind. And the guard at that back entrance is a real goof-off. He's always going in the next room to watch game shows on TV."

"Good deal!" Danny cried. "Maybe we can pick up some CD players and stuff, too, while we're there."

"The only problem is, we can't go in there," Pres told Diane, ignoring his brother. "Reva would recognize us."

"But she wouldn't recognize Danny," Diane said. "Danny could hide in there. He could go up to her, throw a coat over her head or something, and drag her out to us in the car."

"Yeah, I guess," Pres replied reluctantly.

"Whoa. Hold your horses," Danny said, driving with one hand, scratching his oily hair with the other. "I'm not stupid, you know. Do I look stupid to you?"

"Yeah," Pres muttered dryly.

"Well, I'm not stupid," Danny said, scratching his scalp hard. He sped around a slow-moving tractor, nearly sideswiping it. "I'm not kidnapping this girl, doing all the work for a lousy five thousand dollars. No way."

"All right, all right," Pres grumbled. "You can have ten thousand, Danny." He glanced back at Diane to see if she approved.

"Hey—I *told* you—I'm not stupid!" Danny shouted angrily. He slammed the brakes on hard.

Diane cried out. She was nearly thrown up to the

front as the car screeched and skidded wildly across the road.

Pres was thrown against the dashboard. His head bounced off the windshield. "Hey—are you *crazy?"* he screamed at his brother.

The car slid to a stop on the muddy shoulder.

"No way I'm kidnapping her for ten thousand while you guys become millionaires," Danny insisted. "I may look like a jerk, but I'm not."

"Okay. How much do you want?" Pres asked, rubbing his forehead. "How much, Danny?"

"One third," Danny said, staring straight ahead. "We split it three ways. Whatever it is."

Pres turned back to Diane. She shrugged.

"Okay," Pres agreed, frowning. "One third."

"And if the Dalby girl messes me up," Danny said, a strange smile forming on his puffy face, "if she messes me up, I'll kill her. I really will."

Chapter 14

MESSED UP

Reva removed her earring and pressed the phone receiver to her ear. "Hello?" she asked breathlessly.

"Reva? Hi. It's me, Pam. You busy?"

"Well . . . kind of," Reva replied, glancing toward the hallway. She was standing beside the desk in her father's study. Outside the window the night sky was a deep purple-scarlet.

It's going to snow, Reva thought. She shivered. The study was cold. She was eager to get back to the warm fire in the living room.

"I'm really upset," Pam said, her voice thin and shaky on the other end of the line. Pam sneezed. "Sorry."

She's probably up in that drafty little bedroom of hers, Reva thought, shaking her head. Her house is such a dreary place. "What's wrong?" she asked, trying to sound interested.

"It's Victor. He broke our date for tonight," Pam told her. "He said he had to stay home and watch his brother."

"Oh, wow. I've heard *that* excuse before," Reva said sarcastically.

"I called his house a few minutes ago," Pam continued, ignoring her cousin's remark. "And he wasn't there! His brother said he went out."

"Out on a date?" Reva cried. "With who?"

"I—I don't know what to think," Pam stammered. "I really don't."

"You've got to look out for those good-looking ones," Reva said cruelly.

"Huh? What do you mean?" Pam demanded.

"The way he checked me out when we met the other day, I could tell a few things about your friend Victor." Reva smiled to herself, enjoying her little game, deliberately toying with Pam, knowing that she was giving her cousin more to worry about.

Why do I enjoy teasing Pam so much? Reva asked herself. Is it because she's such a perfect victim?

"The way he checked *you* out?" Pam cried shrilly. "What exactly are you saying, Reva? Are you saying that—"

Reva giggled. "No. I'm just saying watch out for him, Pam. Those dark eyes of his—"

"What do *you* know about Victor's eyes?" Pam demanded suspiciously.

Reva giggled. "I know all kinds of things," she replied.

"Reva, are you— I mean, did you— I mean—" Pam sputtered.

Reva's smile grew wider. Torturing Pam was so easy, and so satisfying.

"Reva—if I seriously thought you went out with Victor, I'd die! I really would!" Pam cried, her voice trembling with emotion.

"Calm down, Pam. You're getting crazy. I'm sure everything will work out," Reva replied. "You don't have to start accusing people. He broke only two dates."

"Two dates?" Pam said thoughtfully. "How did you know that? How did you know he broke two? Listen, Reva, if you know something about Victor. . . . If there's something you're not telling me . . ."

"I'm sorry, Pam, I've got to run. Call you later, okay?"

Reva replaced the receiver, a smile on her face, her eyes flashing. Then, eager to get back to the warmth of the fire, she hurried to the living room, brushing back her coppery hair as she walked.

As she entered the room, the firelight sending flickering shadows over the walls, Victor glanced up from the couch. "Who was that?" he asked, motioning for her to return to her place beside him.

"Just a friend," Reva replied.

A few seconds later she was back on the couch, wrapped in Victor's arms, kissing him, kissing him again and again, so cozy and warm before the golden fire.

"Pam would kill me if she ever found out," Victor murmured.

"The old sayings are the best," Reva whispered

into his ear. "What she doesn't know won't hurt her."

She wrapped her hands around his neck and pulled his handsome face to hers.

Poor Pam was so upset. I should tell her that Victor isn't worth it, Reva thought.

Or maybe it would be better to let her find out on her own.

At the same time, less than ten miles away in the neighboring town of Waynesbridge, Diane paced nervously over the threadbare carpet in Pres's dingy apartment. From somewhere down the hall, violin music floated through the thin walls. Diane held her hands over her ears, trying to shut out the whiny sound, trying to think clearly.

Finally, with an exasperated sigh she picked up the receiver of the wall phone in the kitchenette and punched a number with a trembling hand. Waiting for an answer, she rubbed the sleeves of her light cotton sweater, wishing Pres's landlord would send up more heat.

"Hello?" Danny's voice sounded raspy and clogged, as if he had been sleeping.

"Danny, we've got a problem," Diane said, speaking rapidly in a low voice that revealed how upset she felt.

"Huh? Diane? What time is it?" Danny asked groggily.

She glanced at her watch. "It's only ten-fifteen."

"I was getting my beauty sleep," Danny told her. He cleared his throat loudly. "Actually, I got a headache. I was trying to sleep it off. What's up?"

"Your brother messed up," Diane told him, twisting the phone cord around her wrist, leaning against the faded wallpaper.

"Oh, no. What did Pres do? What do you mean, he messed up?" Danny demanded, sounding fully awake now.

"He messed up," Diane repeated with a sigh. "He got himself arrested tonight."

"Huh? For what?" Danny cried. "Jaywalking? Littering?"

"Don't make jokes, Danny," Diane insisted. "Your kid brother got into a fight and beat some guy up. Now he's sitting in the detention center."

Diane waited for Danny to reply, but the line remained silent. "I don't believe this," he said finally. "The stupid jerk."

"I called your parents," Diane continued, winding and unwinding the cord. "They refused to bail him out. They refused to do a thing for him."

"Figures," Danny mumbled.

"And I can't get him out," Diane said. "I don't have a dime."

"Me either," Danny told her.

The violin music grew louder. It seemed to surround Diane. She turned away, stepping into the tiny half-kitchen, trying unsuccessfully to escape from it.

"What about tomorrow?" Danny asked in a low voice. "You know, grabbing the girl."

"I don't know," Diane said, uttering another sigh. "It's such a good idea. And now we can use the money more than ever."

Danny cleared his throat again. "Well, how about

we do it without Pres? You know. Just you and me."

"I guess we could," Diane replied, rubbing her temples. Her hands were cold as ice.

"I'll hide in the stockroom, just like we planned," Danny offered. "And you can drive. You know. Pull up to the loading dock. Keep the engine running. Everything the same. We can do it, Diane. We don't need the stupid jerk."

"Yeah. Okay. I guess." The violin music was driving Diane insane. "Let's do it, Danny. And no slipups this time."

"Yeah. Right," Danny agreed quickly. "No slipups. I told you, I got my headache back. I can't put up with any slipups. Know what I mean?"

Diane felt a chill run down her back as she hung up the receiver. Danny is so unpredictable, so crazy, she thought, not moving away from the wall. When he loses control, he can be really dangerous.

No slipups, she thought.

No slipups.

Maybe bringing Danny into this was a mistake, she thought with a shudder. Maybe it was a big mistake.

Chapter 15

DIANE GETS NERVOUS

Diane eased the car over a speed bump and headed slowly around to the back of Dalby's Department Store. The engine rumbled loudly, making a churning sound that echoed the churning in Diane's stomach.

It has to go right this time, she thought, gripping the wheel tightly. It *has* to. The third time is the charm.

But there were so many things that could go wrong.

What if the car stalled?

What if a security guard saw her parked at a loading dock?

What if Reva didn't show up for her stockroom duties?

What if Danny lost it? What if something got him angry and he exploded? It wouldn't be the first time, Diane thought with a shudder.

She tried to force these questions from her mind, but they kept coming back. Think positive, she kept telling herself.

But she was too nervous to think positive.

Her hands were cold and clammy on the wheel. Her chin was quivering.

Stay cool, Diane. Stay cool. She tried talking herself out of her fear.

When she thought of Pres, sitting in the detention center downtown, her fear turned to anger. How could he do this to Danny and me? she asked herself, biting her lower lip until she tasted blood. How could he leave Danny and me to do all the work?

When Pres comes out, he'll expect his share of the million dollars, Diane thought bitterly. Well, we'll just have to see about that. . . .

It was a bleak gray afternoon. It had snowed the night before, but most of it had melted. A few white clumps dotted the area behind the store.

The old Plymouth let out a choked sound, like a cough. Diane eased the car through a wide, open gate, and the loading area came into view.

Three concrete platforms jutted out from the back of the store. They led to roll-up garage-style doors, all three of which were open. Behind the doors stretched the store's enormous stockroom.

A large yellow truck was backed up to the farthest loading platform. A blue-uniformed driver was closing up the back. Diane could make out the words HOME FURNISHINGS WITH STYLE in red script across the side.

The other two platforms were vacant. Diane searched for security guards, but couldn't see any.

Her heart pounding, she pulled the car up to the middle platform and shifted into Neutral. She leaned across the passenger seat and peered out the window, trying to see into the stockroom.

Danny, are you in there?

Up ahead, the truck driver slammed his door, startling her. She sat up straight, gripping the wheel, and watched as the big yellow truck slowly pulled away.

Good, she thought, a little relieved. Now there's no one else back here, no one to interfere, to mess us up.

She glanced at the dashboard clock, then remembered it was broken.

A loud shot made her cry out and duck. Her heart seemed to leap up from her chest.

She was still trembling all over as she realized the sound came from the home-furnishings truck, backfiring as it pulled away.

I've never been so scared in all my life, Diane realized. She wiped her wet hands on the legs of her jeans.

Danny got the easy job, she thought. She glanced into the rearview mirror, making sure no one was coming up behind her. At least he has something to do. I just have to sit and wait and wait and wait, and be nervous.

What if somebody comes to use the loading

dock? What if a security guard comes? *Then* what do I do?

She pressed her foot down on the gas pedal. The engine rattled, then revved in reply.

She lowered her head to peer into the dark stockroom.

Was Danny in there? Was Reva there?

Was the plan going to work?

Hurry, Danny. Please—hurry!

Diane glanced up again to check the rearview mirror.

And cried out.

A uniformed cop was approaching rapidly, his eyes trained on her car.

Chapter 16

DANNY LOSES CONTROL

Danny leaned against the wooden crate, staying hidden in the deep shadows. He raised his free hand to scratch his hair through the wool ski cap he had pulled down over his face.

On his other arm he had draped the heavy black wool coat he had brought. His plan was to overpower Reva and muffle her cries by throwing the coat over her head. He looked around for the guard, but none was in sight. Lame security, he thought.

As he scratched his head through the hot ski cap, his back began to itch. He rubbed it silently against the wooden crate.

I always itch when I'm nervous, Danny thought. And I'm plenty nervous now.

He had entered the stockroom twenty minutes earlier to find a safe hiding place. Luckily for Danny, a shipment of furniture had just been unloaded. The big crates had been stacked against a wall in the center of the vast stockroom. They gave Danny the perfect place to hide—and to watch for Reva.

So far, so good, he thought, slipping down lower behind the crate as two men walked by, their shoes scraping against the concrete floor.

If only this headache would go away.

The headache was a dull throb at his temples now. Danny closed his eyes and prayed it wouldn't get more intense.

With the headaches came the anger, he knew. The red anger, Danny called it because he always saw flashes of red when the pain got really bad.

The pain made him angry, so angry he sometimes lost control. So angry he seldom remembered what he did.

Danny took a deep breath, then another, willing the headache away.

Reva, where are you? he asked silently, leaning out from behind the tall packing crate.

Reva, don't keep me waiting. Please, don't keep me waiting.

I don't know how long I have . . . until the pain takes over, until the red sweeps over me, takes control of me.

Don't keep me waiting, Reva. For your own good.

Footsteps.

There she is!

He braced himself, every muscle in his body tensed. He straightened the wool ski mask, peering out through the two eyeholes.

The throbbing at his temples grew stronger.

He raised the heavy black coat.

Then lowered it.

It wasn't Reva. It was a middle-aged woman in a tight-fitting gray business suit. Her spike heels clicked loudly on the concrete as she passed.

Danny slumped back against the crate. He was breathing hard now, his breath escaping in noisy gasps. His head itched. He tried to ignore it.

Calm. Be calm.

But the throbbing pain in his head grew sharper, spread down over his eyes.

He closed his eyes, trying to force away the pain.

He could hear voices at one end of the stock-room, someone shouting angrily. Another voice replied, just as angrily.

Shut up. Shut up. Shut up.

He could feel the anger now, the throbbing anger, throbbing with the pain.

He opened his eyes, tried to focus.

But the walls were red. The wooden crates had turned red.

The floor shimmered red, bright red. Throbbing red.

Fight it down. Fight it down, Danny told himself.

This had been happening so often to him lately. First the pain, then the red anger.

Maybe I should see a doctor, he thought. He pressed his hands against the pulsing.

And then she was there.

Reva. Wearing a long white sweater over black leggings. Carrying a stack of small packages.

Yes.

Danny squinted through the bright red, saw her clearly. Saw her come near. Nearer.

Yes!

The pain shot through him. It felt as if someone were tightening a thick rubber band around the top of his head. Tighter. Tighter.

Glaring into the red, he crept up behind her.

He raised the black wool coat.

I've got you now, he thought, struggling against the pain, against the rage that roared through every muscle.

I've got you now, Reva.

I hope I don't have to do anything terrible.

Chapter 17
GOTCHA!

Staring into the rearview mirror, Diane watched the grim-faced officer approach. He had his dark blue cap pulled low over his forehead. His hands were in gloves, one resting on the handle of his nightstick, the other swinging at his side.

This isn't happening, Diane thought, her throat choked with panic. She forced herself to start breathing again.

This *can't* be happening.

Oh, please. Please—walk by the car. Keep right on walking. *Please.*

But no. He tapped on her window.

Diane reached for the knob and lowered the window halfway, her entire body shaking. Her chin quivered, out of control. She wondered if he could see it.

"What are you doing here, miss?" he asked. His voice was high and thin. It didn't match his heavy body or hard, solemn face at all.

"Uh . . . nothing." She couldn't think straight. She could barely speak.

She glanced toward the loading dock.

What if Danny came running out with the girl right now?

They'd both be caught.

"Why are you parked here?" the officer asked, lowering his head to the window, his gray-green eyes exploring the front seat of the car.

"Uh . . . I'm waiting for someone," Diane managed to choke out.

She glanced at the wide doors again. *Don't come out, Danny. Don't come out now.*

"I'm sorry," the officer said, frowning. "You'll have to move."

"He'll be out in a minute," Diane insisted in a trembling voice. "Really."

"There's a parking lot over there," he said, pointing a black glove in the direction Diane had come. "You'll have to wait there."

"But, sir—?"

"Sorry." His eyes narrowed at her. "There's no waiting back here. Move it. Now."

Fighting back the waves of pain at his temples, Danny lifted the heavy coat in both hands.

The floor shimmered like a pool of water. Red then gray. Red then gray.

Moving quickly, Danny crept up behind her.

She stopped suddenly.

He nearly bumped into her.

Swallowing hard, struggling to see through the curtain of red, he pulled the coat down over her head.

Her arms shot up. The boxes she'd been carrying fell noisily to the floor.

Danny glanced around. No one in sight.

She tried to scream, but he wrapped the coat tightly over her face. Her cry came out a muffled whimper.

She twisted and squirmed.

He gave her a hard shove forward, wrapping his arm around the coat, holding it tight around her head.

"Don't fight me!" he murmured, surprised at his own fury. "Don't fight me!"

But she bent in half, trying to duck out from under the coat. Her arms flailed. She uttered another muffled cry of protest.

"Stop it!" Danny cried in a loud, angry whisper. He shot his fist into her back.

She gasped, startled by the pain.

It took her only a few seconds to recover. Then she tried spinning around, twisting out of his grip.

The coat started to slip.

Danny leaned against her, holding the coat down over her. He drove his free hand hard into her back again. He pushed her toward the open door, shoving with his shoulder, holding on to the coat.

She stiffened her legs, tried to push back. Her shoes skidded against the concrete.

"Stop it! Stop it!" Danny cried furiously, feeling

himself losing control. "You want to get hurt? I'll hurt you!"

One hard blow knocked the girl unconscious.

Then, wrapping the coat tightly over her upper body, Danny held her around the waist and dragged her to the car.

Chapter 18

MILLIONAIRES

The officer glared at Diane. "Did you hear me?"

Diane stared back at him, frantically thinking. What can I do? she asked herself. I can't leave this spot. If Danny comes out dragging Reva, and I'm not here . . .

"My . . . uh . . . father is very sick," she stammered. "He works here. In the stockroom. I have to take him to the hospital. That's why I stopped back here. He'll be out in one second. If you'll only let me—"

"You can wait over there, young lady," the officer interrupted. "I'm getting a little tired of repeating myself. Now, put the car in gear and pull over to the lot. Don't make me write out a ticket."

Diane swallowed hard. Her throat felt as if it were clogged with sand. "Sorry, sir."

She glanced to the platform. No sign of Danny. Thank goodness. Reluctantly, she started to shift the car into gear.

I can't believe this is happening, she thought miserably. I can't believe our plans are being messed up for a third time.

A wave of sadness swept over her.

Loser. The word flared into her mind. I'm a loser.

Pres and Danny and I, we're all losers.

Slowly, with the police officer still hovering over the car, she began to pull away.

A loud crash—the crunch of metal hitting metal, followed by shattering glass—made her stop.

"Oh, no!" she cried.

At first Diane thought she had hit something. It took her a second to realize the crash had come from the parking lot.

She heard angry voices. Shouts and curses.

"I've got to go over there!" the officer shouted, reaching for his nightstick. "You be gone when I get back—hear?"

Diane stuck her head out the window, watching him run toward the shouting voices.

"Yes!" she cried gleefully. Some luck. Some good luck. She finally had some good luck.

She jumped when the back door suddenly swung open. "Hey—" She had been so involved with the police officer, she hadn't watched for Danny.

"Go! Go! Go!" he shouted.

She turned to the backseat to see him shove Reva into the car. The heavy coat was draped over Reva's head. She didn't move.

What has he done to her? Diane wondered. "Danny, did you—?"

"Just knocked her out," Danny replied, breathing hard.

Danny shoved Reva across the seat and slid in beside her. He kept his arm around her shoulder, holding the coat over her. "Go! Go! Go!" he repeated, slamming the car door, then leaning close to Reva, pressing her against the seatback in case she came to.

"I don't believe it! You . . . got her!" Diane cried.

"Shut up and drive!" Danny raged.

Gripping the wheel tightly with both hands, Diane pulled away from the platform. The car shot forward as she plunged her foot all the way down on the gas pedal and turned toward the street.

Glancing in the rearview mirror, she searched for the policeman. She had a frightening vision of him chasing after them.

But there was no one.

She pulled onto the street, the threadbare tires squealing, and turned toward the highway that led to Waynesbridge.

"We did it!" she cried gleefully. "I don't believe it! We did it!"

Danny grinned at her, still holding the coat tightly over Reva's head. "We're going to be millionaires!" he exclaimed. "Millionaires!"

"Just like in the movies!" Diane declared.

If only Pres could be here, she thought, feeling a twinge of sadness. If only Pres could enjoy this too.

But soon they would get Pres out. Soon Pres would be back with them.

And they would be rich, richer than they had ever dreamed.

Christmas was almost here. What a great Christmas it was going to be.

Millionaires. That's what we'll be—millionaires, Diane thought, so excited she drove through a stop sign.

Dalby will gladly fork over a million to get his precious daughter back.

We've done it! Just like in the movies!

And now nothing can go wrong.

Nothing.

Chapter 19

A SLIGHT PROBLEM

"I think we've made Dalby squirm enough," Diane said, taking the last bite of her peanut butter sandwich.

Danny chuckled. He tossed down the old copy of *Sports Illustrated* he'd been flipping through. "Yeah. We've had the girl here a full day," he said, gesturing to the bedroom. "I'll bet Dalby's squirming."

"I wanted to wait at least twenty-four hours," Diane said, carrying the plate over to the small sink and running cold water over it. "Sometimes rich people are so busy making money, they don't know if their family is missing or not."

Danny pushed himself up from the chair and stretched, a bulge of white belly showing under his olive-colored pullover. "One day is enough. Dalby is probably waiting by the phone, sweating bullets, waiting for our call."

"I hope so," Diane said, setting the dish beside the sink. She dried her hands on a paper towel. "Dalby's daughter is a total pain."

"Yeah. Can you imagine? She won't eat and she won't say a word," Danny said, shaking his head.

"She *better* not say a word!" Diane exclaimed, shooting him a nervous glance. "You tightened the gag, right?"

Danny nodded. "I checked everything. She's tied up, blindfolded, and gagged. The works."

"Just make sure she doesn't work the gag loose. I don't want a sound coming out of her," Diane said, pulling on her coat. "You know how thin the walls are in this dump."

"Guess you'll be moving into a big, fancy house," Danny said, teasing her. "With a maid and a butler and a chauffeur."

Diane didn't find his remarks amusing. "I won't be eighteen for another four months," she told him. "I've got to keep the money a secret until then, or my parents will try to grab it."

Danny *tsk-tsk*ed. "Where you going? I thought you were going to call Dalby and tell him how he can get his daughter back."

"I am," she replied sharply. "But you don't expect me to call from here, do you? They'll trace the call and pick us up in ten minutes flat!"

Danny turned his glance to the window. "Yeah. I knew that. I was just testing you." He picked up the *Sports Illustrated.* "Know what I'm going to do when I get my share? I'm going to get a tattoo."

"You always had a lot of class," Diane said dryly. She zipped her coat and started to the door.

"Wonder why we haven't heard from Pres," Danny muttered, his face buried in the magazine.

"Shh. No names!" Diane said sharply, motioning to the bedroom. "I wonder too." She stopped with her hand on the doorknob. "Hope he didn't get into more trouble in the detention center."

"Maybe they found out about that car he stole," Danny said.

"Huh?" Diane turned around in surprise. "I never heard about that."

Danny blushed. He avoided her stare. "Oh. Well. He only borrowed it for a little bit. He didn't really steal it."

Diane laughed. "Well, he could have offered *me* a ride in it! I'm getting sick of the old Plymouth."

"You can buy five cars," Danny muttered. "After we trade Reva in."

Diane glanced toward the bedroom. "Just keep an eye on her, Danny. I know you plan to take a nap the minute I leave. But watch her, okay? We don't want any slipups now, you know?"

"Yeah. Okay, okay," he growled, scratching his head. "I'll watch her. Go make the call already. I'm getting old, sitting here."

Diane made her way out the door, closing it carefully behind her. She stepped out into a bright, clear day that felt more like September than December. The ground was spotted with patches of old snow, one of the few signs that it was winter.

She bent to pet the head of an old hound dog that always hung around the apartment building. "Who do you belong to?" she asked it, rubbing its damp fur. "Or do you own this joint?" The old dog wagged its tail slowly in reply.

Diane climbed into the car. It took three tries to get the engine to grind to a start. Then she headed to the Division Street Mall, where she planned to find a secluded phone booth to make her call.

The car radio was broken, but Diane didn't need it. She hummed happily to herself, tapping her hands on the wheel, rehearsing for the thousandth time in her mind what she planned to say to Mr. Dalby.

Robert Dalby, Reva's father, shifted uncomfortably in his armchair. He lowered his copy of the *Wall Street Journal* and stared into the fireplace, watching the flames jump and dance.

With a weary sigh he picked up the newspaper and began to read again.

When the phone on the table beside him rang, he let out a startled cry. He fumbled for the receiver, knocking over his small glass of sherry.

The liquid formed a brown puddle on the polished tabletop. Ignoring it, Mr. Dalby managed to grab up the receiver on the second ring. "Hello?"

"Is this Robert Dalby?" A young woman's voice.

"Yes. Speaking."

"Mr. Dalby," said the young woman, very stern

and businesslike, "I . . . uh . . . I have your daughter. She's okay and everything. I . . . I called to tell you what you need to do to get her back. It will cost you a million dollars, see. Don't worry. We have your daughter, safe and sound."

"No, you don't," Robert Dalby replied. "My daughter, Reva, is sitting right here with me."

Chapter 20

NOT REVA

Mr. Dalby stared into the fire as he listened to the gasp on the other end. He could hear voices in the background, the clink of plates and silverware. The caller must be in a restaurant somewhere, he realized.

He struggled to recognize the voice.

Was it a voice he had heard before? Was it a girl who had worked for him? Who still worked for him?

He didn't recognize her. All he could tell was that she was nervous. And young.

Reva had gotten up from her chair by the fire and stood beside him, listening to his conversation. "Daddy—?"

Mr. Dalby raised a finger to silence her.

Reva placed an arm on the back of her father's

chair and leaned close, trying to hear the voice on the other end.

"Mr. Dalby, would you repeat what you just said?" Diane demanded in a trembling voice.

She stood in a narrow phone booth at the back of the Doughnut Hole restaurant at the Division Street Mall. The door to the booth would close only halfway, so she stood with her back to the restaurant.

"I said that my daughter, Reva, is home with me," Mr. Dalby repeated gruffly.

In the cramped phone booth Diane shuddered. The walls closed in on her. Everything went dark. A heavy feeling of cold dread made her feel as if she were about to faint.

Or scream.

Was Dalby telling the truth?

Was he trying some kind of stupid trick?

"Mr. Dalby, don't play games with us," she managed to say in a tight, shrill voice.

"Whoever you are, listen to me!" Robert Dalby shouted.

"Mr. Dalby—"

"Let that girl go!" Dalby sputtered into the phone. "That girl is not my daughter. You will not get a *penny* from me. You have kidnapped the wrong girl!"

PART TWO

ANOTHER KIDNAPPING

Chapter 21

"WE HAVE TO KILL HER"

Pam had been struggling against the cords that bound her wrists. But her efforts only made them cut deeper into her skin.

She let her body go limp and struggled to slow her breathing. Pain shot up her legs from where her ankles were tightly tied. Her throat ached behind the gag.

Where am I? Why are they keeping me here so long?

What are they going to do to me?

The questions wouldn't go away. As hard as she struggled to force them from her mind, they kept coming back. And with the questions came a rising panic that choked her and sent shiver after cold shiver down her body.

Why did they kidnap me? What do they want with ME?

All at once Pam knew the answer to those questions.

They didn't want me. They wanted Reva. My millionaire cousin.

Reva. Reva. Reva.

The name burned more cruelly than the pain at her wrists and ankles.

This is Reva's fault, Pam thought bitterly. This *has* to be Reva's fault.

No one would want to kidnap me. They *had* to want Reva.

Reva. Reva. Reva.

Pam repeated the name until it became an ugly chant.

And now will I have to DIE because of Reva?

A tingling sensation crept up her back. It felt as if a thousand tiny insects were crawling all over her.

Pam tried to swallow, but her throat was too dry. If they don't loosen this gag, I'm going to choke to death, she thought.

For the thousandth time she rubbed her head against the pillow, trying to slide the blindfold off. But it wouldn't budge.

Reva. Reva. Reva.

They wanted Reva. But they got me.

Pam could hear the two of them fighting about it in the next room. There was a girl and a guy, she knew that much.

She hadn't been able to catch their names. They

had been very careful about not saying their names. The girl sounded young, Pam thought. A teenager, maybe. The guy—she couldn't tell. He was loud and vulgar, and he always sounded angry.

He sounded very angry now. They were moving around noisily in the other room, pacing back and forth.

Pam struggled to hear their conversation.

"It's not my fault!" the girl was shrieking.

"Not my fault. Not my fault!" The guy nastily imitated her voice. "Then whose fault is it, honey-bunch?"

"You and Pres went to the store. You went right up to her, didn't you?" the man demanded.

"Please—no names!" the girl protested. "She can hear us. You know how thin the walls are."

"So tell me how it happened," the man insisted, ignoring her complaint. "How did we get the wrong girl? How could you not know?"

"I never saw her face!" the girl screamed shrilly. "I was down on the floor, pretending to search for my contact, remember? I never saw her. She was wearing some kind of big floppy hat!"

The man let out a snarl of rage. Then Pam heard a crash. The girl screamed. Had he thrown a lamp or something at her?

"The neighbors! The neighbors!" she was screaming now, her voice high with fright.

Maybe they'll let me go, Pam thought. She felt a sharp stab of pain at her ankles. The cords were too tight. Too tight. Her feet were tingling, numb.

Now that they know they have the wrong girl, maybe they'll let me go.

She held her breath, listening hard. It was quiet in the other room now.

"I'm sick," the man whined. "I'm really sick. All this work. All this . . . tension."

"It's a stupid mix-up," the girl replied. "If your stupid brother had been with us—"

"I'm sick," the man repeated. "My headache is coming back. I can feel it."

"How do you think *I* feel?" the girl cried emotionally. "This was supposed to be a great Christmas. It was supposed to be like in the movies. But now . . ."

Now *what?* Pam wondered. *What?*

Now what are you going to do? Let me go home? Please, oh, please—let me go home!

Pam heard footsteps in the next room, the floor creaking.

"Let's go see who she is," the man was saying. "Maybe we've got someone good in there. You know. Another rich girl."

No, you don't, Pam thought miserably. You don't have a rich girl. You've got Reva Dalby's poor cousin.

Her heart jumped as she heard the door open. She heard footsteps approaching the bed. A stab of pain shot out from her cut wrists. The tingling crept up her back.

They're in the room. They're looking at me.

What are they going to do to me?

She tried to make a sound, but her throat was too dry, the gag too tight.

Suddenly she felt the pressure of hands on her face. The gag was untied and pulled off.

"Who *are* you?" the man called down to her. "What's your name?"

She opened her mouth but realized she couldn't make a sound. *"Water,"* she managed to whisper. *"Water, please."*

"What's your name?" he insisted impatiently.

"Get her a glass of water," the girl urged.

"Please," Pam pleaded.

A few moments later she felt a hand push her head up from the back. Then she felt the rim of a glass pushed up to her parched lips.

The water was lukewarm. She choked on it at first, then managed to get a few swallows. It felt good on her throat. She drank thirstily. Water ran down her chin.

She wanted more, but the glass was taken away. Her head fell back onto the pillow. Pain rolled up her legs. Tingling pain.

"Please untie me. It hurts," she choked out.

"No way," the man growled. "Your name!"

"What are you going to do to me?" Pam cried shrilly.

"Your name!"

"Are you going to hurt me? What are you going to do?"

"Don't hit her!" the girl suddenly cried.

Pam let out a frightened cry. She sucked in her breath, expecting to be struck.

But the girl spoke instead, close to Pam's ear. "We're not going to hurt you if you cooperate," she said softly. "We need to know your name."

"Pam," Pam told her softly. "Pam Dalby." There was no point in lying.

"Dalby?" the man cried, sounding surprised. "You're a Dalby?"

"I don't believe this!" the girl exclaimed.

"Untie me," Pam pleaded, feeling about to cry. "My legs, they're numb. Everything hurts."

"Tough break," the man replied nastily. "Are you Reva Dalby's sister?"

Reva. Reva. Reva.

Pam shook her head. She felt two hot tears run down her cheeks.

"You're *not* her sister?" the man demanded suspiciously.

"N-no," Pam stammered. "I'm her cousin."

There was a heavy silence. Then Pam heard the man say "Bingo. Reva Dalby's cousin. Maybe our luck is changing."

"Let me go!" Pam cried, feeling more hot tears trickle down her cheeks. "Please—you've got to let me go!"

They ignored her. "Don't you think Dalby would pay big to get his niece back?" the man was asking the girl.

"No!" Pam blurted out. "He won't pay for me. Our families aren't close. I know him. He won't pay! Please—just let me go!" She began to sob loudly.

Over her sobs Pam could hear the two of them discussing her, talking excitedly in loud whispers.

"I wish your brother were here. He'd know what to do," the girl said tensely.

"Is she lying?" the man demanded.

"I don't think so," the girl replied. "I think she's

telling the truth. I don't think we can get a dime for her."

There was a long silence.

Then Pam heard the words she'd been dying to hear. "Maybe we should just let her go," the girl said.

"Huh? Let her go?" The man reacted with angry disbelief. "No way. Uh-uh. No way! We can't let her go. We have no choice. We have to kill her."

Chapter 22

KILLED

Reva clicked her long nails against the smooth desktop, holding the cordless phone between her chin and shoulder. She glanced across her bedroom to the clock radio beside her bed. Nine forty-three at night.

"I feel so guilty," Victor was saying at the other end of the line. "I just feel so horribly guilty."

"Why should *you* feel guilty?" Reva demanded, sounding more irritated than sympathetic. "*You* didn't kidnap Pam!"

"But I—" Victor hesitated. "I was with you, Reva, when—"

"I could have been kidnapped," Reva interrupted. She tugged down the sleeves of her pale blue cashmere sweater. "Can you imagine? It was supposed to be me! If I hadn't convinced Pam to take my shift in the stockroom, it would have been me! What a thought! I get chills every time I think about it."

"Can't you think about Pam for once?" Victor replied sharply.

"Of course. I feel terrible for her," Reva said unconvincingly. She raised the back of her hand and studied her nails.

"Have you heard from the kidnappers? Did they call again?" Victor asked.

"Not since yesterday," Reva replied. "The FBI hasn't a clue as to who it is. Not a clue."

"How about your father?" Victor asked. "Does he have any ideas? Did he recognize the girl's voice?"

"I don't think so."

"Does he have money ready to pay the kidnappers?" Victor asked.

"No way," Reva replied.

"Huh?" Victor uttered a surprise gasp.

"Daddy won't pay. He doesn't believe in paying kidnappers. He says it only encourages other kidnappers."

"He won't pay to get his own niece back?" Victor cried.

"Daddy has very strict principles," Reva said flatly. "He isn't here. He had an emergency and had to fly to his store in Walnut Creek. He won't be back till tomorrow."

"You're all alone there?" Victor's voice was high with his surprise.

"My dad made sure the police send a patrol car around every half hour to check on me," Reva told him.

Reva liked it better when Victor worried about her instead of moaning about how guilty he felt and how worried he was about Pam. She felt bad about Pam. Pam was her only cousin, after all. But Reva was certain the kidnappers would let Pam go as soon as they realized they wouldn't get a penny for her.

"I—I *am* kind of frightened, Victor," she said, putting on her little girl voice. "I mean, the kidnappers were after *me*, after all. I start *shaking* every time I think how close I came to being kidnapped."

"What a nightmare," Victor said earnestly.

She could just picture the serious, concerned look in his dark eyes. Victor is so good-looking, Reva thought with a sigh. But he's basically a dim bulb. Very low wattage in the brain area.

What a shame, she thought, flipping through a copy of *Sassy* as she talked with him. I never dreamed I'd grow tired of him so quickly.

"Would you like me to come over?" Victor asked. "Would you feel safer?"

Reva laughed. "Who would protect me from *you?*"

Victor didn't laugh. "No. Really," he insisted. "I could be there in ten minutes."

"I'll be okay," Reva told him. "Hey—I forgot to tell you about my dream. It was so weird. So scary."

"You dreamed about Pam?" Victor guessed.

"No. Well, sort of," Reva replied, closing the

magazine. She shifted the cordless phone to her other shoulder. "It woke me up last night. It was very disturbing. I was shopping. In the dream, I mean."

"Shopping?"

"Yeah. In some kind of big department store," Reva continued. "Maybe it was my dad's store. I don't know. I didn't really recognize it. When the dream started, the store was very crowded, very bright and noisy. I was walking from aisle to aisle, pushing through the crowds. It was very unpleasant. I remember I didn't like it at all. But I just kept walking.

"The store seemed endless, aisle after aisle," Reva continued. "I wanted to leave, but I couldn't find a door. Then, suddenly, it grew very quiet. Silent. I looked around. The store was empty. No one there. Except me. Me and someone else. I heard footsteps behind me, and I knew someone was chasing me. You know how you just know things in dreams?"

"Yeah. Sure," Victor replied. "Scary."

"Wait. It gets worse," Reva promised. "I started to run. I was searching for an exit, any exit. But there was only aisle after aisle. I was terrified. I ran. Ran through the aisles. But he was right behind me. Getting closer. Closer. The only sounds were his footsteps and my panting breaths. I ran and ran. It seemed like I ran forever.

"And then he grabbed me," Reva said.

"Who?" Victor demanded breathlessly.

"He had me by the shoulders," she continued. "He wanted to drag me away, to kidnap me. I knew he wanted to kidnap me. But I fought and spun away. I turned around to see who it was. And—it was Santa Claus!"

"Huh?"

Reva laughed. "It was Santa Claus. Do you believe it? Ho-ho-ho!"

"Weird!" Victor exclaimed. "Then what happened?"

"I woke up," Reva told him.

Victor didn't say anything for a long while. Reva could almost hear his brain whirring. "I guess you were worried about Pam," he offered finally.

"Yeah, I guess," Reva replied, yawning. "I never can figure out what my dreams mean. I only know it was weird."

"You sure you don't want me to come over?" he asked.

Before Reva could answer, she heard a loud noise outside. She recognized the sound immediately—a car door slamming.

"Victor, I've got to get off. Someone's here," she told him. She jumped up and carried the phone to her bedroom window.

Pushing back the curtains, she peered down to the driveway. She heard the squeal of tires. A car roared away. But she couldn't see it.

What *was* that thing at the bottom of the driveway? Was it a large sack? A garbage bag? She squinted hard, trying to see.

"Who is it?" Victor was asking.

"I don't know. I'll call you later." She turned off the phone and tossed it onto her bed.

Then she hurried down the carpeted stairs, taking them two at a time. Opening the coat closet, she grabbed a down jacket. She pulled it over her shoulders as she opened the front door, leapt outside, and began running to the bottom of the driveway.

It was a clear, cold night. Her breath steamed up in front of her as she ran. Newly installed spotlights in the trees cast white cones of light over the front lawn.

Reva gasped as she neared the street.

Lying in the driveway, sprawled on her back. A body.

A girl's body.

Pam!

Panting loudly, Reva dropped to her knees beside her cousin.

"Oh, no," she moaned. "They *killed* her."

Chapter 23

FOOTSTEPS

Pam's eyes were closed. Her hair fell in a tangled disarray beneath her head. Her skin was gray under the pale wash of light from the lights overhead in the trees.

"They killed her," Reva murmured. She swallowed hard. Her throat suddenly felt dry. A chill ran down her back.

Glancing up, she saw a low, dark form racing across the frozen grass toward her. She jumped to her feet, then realized it was only King, her guard dog.

The big dog lowered its head and let out a soft, whimpering sound.

"It's okay, King," Reva said, her voice tiny and frightened. "It's okay, fella. Get lost. Get lost, King."

The dog stared at her for a moment, its eyes red in the eerie light. Then it sat on its haunches on the edge of the driveway.

Reva heard a low groan. She lowered her eyes to the driveway.

Pam blinked. Once. Twice. She groaned again. Her eyes opened. She stared up blankly at Reva.

"Pam!" Reva cried. She dropped back down beside her cousin. "Pam! You're—alive!"

Pam struggled to raise her head. But the effort proved to be too much for her. Wincing in pain, she closed her eyes and lowered her head back to the driveway.

"You're alive!" Reva repeated. She cradled Pam's head in her hands. She stroked Pam's damp, tangled hair.

"I'm not so sure," Pam groaned.

"We've got to get you inside," Reva said, shivering. "Do you think you can stand up?"

"Let's give it a try," Pam replied shakily. "I-I've been tied up. My legs, they were completely numb."

Reva helped pull Pam slowly to her feet. Then, allowing Pam to lean on her, Reva slipped an arm around her cousin's waist and guided her up the driveway to the house.

"They—they knocked me out. I was just coming to when they *heaved* me out of the car," Pam said as Reva lowered her onto the dark leather couch in the den. "I hit my head on the pavement. I guess I blacked out again."

"Lie down on the pillows," Reva instructed Pam,

moving a soft satiny pillow behind Pam's head. "That's it. I'll get you a glass of water."

"Thanks," Pam said, shutting her eyes. "I-I'm still a little dazed, I think. I'm very shaky. You know? Everything's trembling. My heart is racing."

"I'll call Dr. Simms," Reva said, heading toward the kitchen. "And your parents. They'll be so happy!" And then she added, "I'll call the FBI too. I have their number right by the phone. And the Shadyside police."

Reva hurried to the kitchen. She filled a glass with cold water from the dispenser in the refrigerator door.

As she started to return to the den, she cried out, startled to find Pam right behind her. "Hey—you scared me!"

"Sorry," Pam murmured, lowering her green eyes.

"You should lie down, Pam."

"I don't want to be alone," Pam said fretfully. "I'm so . . . shaky. I'll just sit down at the counter." She pulled out a wooden kitchen stool and climbed onto it.

"What happened?" Reva asked, watching Pam gulp the water. "How did you get away?"

"They had a big fight over what to do with me," Pam replied, working nervously at the tangles in her hair with one hand. "There were two of them."

"Yeah? Did you get a good look at them?" Reva asked, leaning her hands on the white counter.

"No." Pam shook her head solemnly. "They had me blindfolded the whole time. I only heard their voices."

"Did you hear their names?" Reva asked eagerly.

Pam shook her head again. "No. They were careful."

"Did they beat you up or anything?" Reva asked, her face tightening with concern as she studied Pam carefully.

"It—it was *horrible!"* Pam cried in a trembling voice. "I was so scared, Reva. They threw a coat over me and hit me hard on the head. In the stockroom. When I woke up I was in a bed somewhere. All tied up. Blindfolded and gagged. I—I thought they were going to kill me. I really did."

"Take it easy, Pam," Reva said softly.

Pam let out a sob, her skin pale in the kitchen light. "The man, he really wanted to kill me. He was very hotheaded, angry all the time. Really out of control. The girl sounded too frightened to kill me. She just wanted to get rid of me. They argued and argued.

"Finally they decided to dump me on your driveway and leave town as fast as possible," Pam continued.

"They left town?" Reva's expression was one of surprise mixed with relief.

"Yeah. They're gone," Pam said. "I heard them say they had a friend in Canada. They were going to go up there and lay low for a while."

Pam smiled for the first time. "I'm so glad. I'm so glad they're gone, Reva." Her shoulders shook. She lowered her head into her hands and started to cry.

Reva hurried over and put a calming hand on her cousin's trembling shoulder. "You're okay now,

Pam," she whispered. "You're okay. They're gone. And you're okay."

Pam was still crying softly when Reva heard the footsteps.

Heavy footsteps in the front hall.

Oh, no! Reva thought, raising a hand to her mouth. *I left the front door wide open!*

The footsteps grew louder.

Pam heard them too.

She jerked her head up, her eyes wild with fear. "They came back!" she cried in a choked whisper.

Chapter 24

WHO'S WATCHING REVA?

Both girls froze, their eyes locked on each other as they listened.

The footsteps were in the back hall now.

Pam uttered a low gasp, her shoulders still trembling.

Reva pulled a copper frying pan off its hook on the wall. Gripping the handle tightly, she held it high, preparing to use it as a weapon.

The footsteps drew closer. Closer.

From the hallway Reva heard heavy breathing.

"Who—who's there?" she managed to stammer.

A few seconds later Victor appeared in the kitchen doorway. At first he saw only Reva. Gesturing to the hall, his eyes narrowed in confusion. "The front door—it was wide open," he said. "I was worried—"

"Victor!" Pam cried. She dropped down from the stool.

"Pam! I don't believe it! You—you're okay!" Victor's handsome face showed surprise, then happiness. He ran across the room and wrapped his arms around Pam, and they hugged.

A happy ending for all, Reva thought, watching them. Pam is so innocent. She doesn't even wonder why Victor came over here.

This works out fine, Reva thought, a pleased smile crossing her face as she watched Pam and Victor hold each other. This saves me the trouble of dumping Victor.

"Hey, break it up, you two!" Reva cried. "We've got to call Pam's parents!"

On Saturday afternoon Reva got a postcard from St. Croix from her brother, Michael. On the front was a white beach shaded by palm trees. On the back Michael had printed:

> We took a boat and went snorkeling at Buck Island. Then Josh and I rode the waves into the beach for two hours! My bathing suit got filled with sand. I miss you. NOT!

Reva stared at the palm trees. It looked like a nice beach. She imagined the sound of the soft waves rolling onto the sand. She pictured the turquoise water. She could almost smell the coconut suntan lotion.

"That little creep Michael has all the luck!" Reva cried bitterly.

She glanced out the living room window. The sky was nearly as dark as night. A freezing rain was being blown in all directions by a howling, swirling wind.

Reva sighed. It's the Saturday before Christmas, she thought wistfully. I have no choice. I have to go out and buy presents.

Pulling on her hooded poncho, she made her way to the garage. Then she drove her red Miata to the Division Street Mall.

The storm hadn't kept the shoppers at home. Reva had to circle the underground parking garage three times before she found a place to park.

She pushed her way impatiently through the crowded stores. The smell of wet wool filled the air. Babies were crying. People juggled bulging shopping bags and umbrellas. Everyone looks so rain soaked and bedraggled, she thought.

Bouncy Christmas music jangled from loudspeakers in every store. Reva wandered into a long, narrow shop called The Cozy Corner. It had an entire wall of earrings, mostly plastic and glass.

Reva knew she would never shop in a store like this for herself. But when it came to buying presents for others, she never liked to spend a lot of money.

She stared at the wall of earrings. These earrings are all so tacky, Reva thought, examining a pair shaped like little Hershey bars. But they're perfect for Pam.

She saw plastic earrings shaped like food. She picked up a pair of peanut-butter-sandwich earrings, then quickly replaced them.

Moving sideways, she made her way down the long display. A pair of plastic banana earrings caught her eye. No, she thought. Those are too gross, even for Pam.

Reva was nearly to the end of the display wall when she noticed a dark-haired man in a black trench coat. He was standing a few yards away, leaning against a low display case filled with silver and plastic bracelets.

His round, blue-lensed sunglasses caught the light. Hands shoved in his trench coat pockets, he had been staring at Reva, but he glanced away immediately when she stared back at him.

His straight black hair fell over his forehead. He was good-looking, Reva thought. He looked a little like Elvis Presley. She wondered what his eyes were like behind the blue shades.

He doesn't seem to be shopping, Reva observed. Maybe he's waiting for someone.

She bought a pair of long, dangly glass earrings, paying for them with her American Express card. Then she made her way out to the center court to look for a menswear store.

A nice, boring tie for Dad, she thought, ducking out of the way of a swinging umbrella. Poor Dad. He spends a fortune for his clothes. But everything he buys is so dull and conservative.

A few moments later she was sifting through a

table of ties at Brooks Brothers. Gazing up, she was surprised to see the guy in the blue sunglasses again. He stood outside the store, staring in at her through the window.

Why is he looking at me like that? Reva wondered.

And then she had a chilling thought: Is he following me?

No. No way. She scolded herself for being so jumpy.

You're still a little freaked because of Pam, she told herself. But you've got to cool it, Reva. Just because you see the same guy twice doesn't mean he's following you.

And just because he's staring into a store window doesn't mean he's staring at *you.*

As she handed a blue- and black-striped tie and her American Express card to the clerk at the cash register, she glanced warily to the window. The young man was gone.

See? she thought, feeling foolish. You scared yourself for no reason.

But a few minutes later, as she was examining blouses at Silk Casuals, she saw him again. He stood a few aisles away, hands in his trench coat pockets, head lowered, black hair falling over the front of his blue glasses.

He *is* staring at me, Reva realized. I'm not imagining it.

He followed her to CD World.

Walking fast, bumping people out of her way, she tried to lose him in the crowd at the Food Court. But glancing back, she saw him steadily making his way toward her, keeping his distance, his dark glasses trained on her.

As she hurried down to the parking garage, Reva realized she was trembling all over.

Who is he—one of the kidnappers? she wondered.

Did they tell Pam they were going to Canada just to throw everyone off? To make us lower our guard?

She kept glancing nervously behind her, her boots clicking loudly on the hard concrete floor as she started to run through the rows of parked cars.

Did they lie to Pam?

Are they following *me* now?

Are they planning to grab *me* next?

Chapter 25

BIG SURPRISE AT PAM'S

Reva tapped her long purple fingernails on the glass perfume counter. She raised her eyes to a woman who had been trying to get her attention for nearly five minutes. Look at the nose on this woman, Reva thought scornfully. You could hang a coat on it. Haven't you ever heard of plastic surgery, lady?

"Can you recommend a fragrance?" the woman asked, smiling anxiously at Reva. "Something different. My husband is tired of my old fragrance."

Then maybe you should take a bath, Reva thought. She almost burst out laughing. I really crack myself up, she told herself.

"Try this one. It's brand-new," Reva said, picking up a small sample spray bottle. "Hold up your wrist." Or should I just spray it on your nose?

She sprayed a mist of the cologne on the woman's wrist. The woman sniffed it, tilting her head in concentration.

Don't sniff too hard, Reva thought. You could inhale your entire arm!

"It's very flowery," the woman said. She sniffed again. "I like it." She lowered her wrist, smiling at Reva. "What's it called?"

It's called Eau de Skunk, Reva thought.

"It's called Black Rose," she said. Gazing beyond the woman, she saw Pam making her way through the crowded aisle.

"Well, could you tell me the price?" the woman asked, sniffing her wrist again.

"Not right now," Reva said, her eyes on Pam. She pointed to Francine, who was handling three other customers at the far end of the counter. "She'll help you. I've got to run."

"But—but—miss?"

As the woman sputtered her protest, Reva hurried away to meet Pam. "Hey, Pam—you're back at work?"

Pam nodded, smiling at Reva. She wore a short black dress over dark green tights. Her blond hair was tied behind her head in a ponytail.

"I can't believe you came back so soon," Reva exclaimed. "Why didn't you take a few more days to rest and get your head together?"

"I couldn't," Pam replied, lowering her gaze. "I really need the money."

"Don't they have kidnapping pay or something?" Reva demanded. That was a thoughtless thing to say, she thought. Pam has been through a really terrifying time, and here I am making dumb jokes about it.

"Talk to Uncle Robert about that," Pam replied dryly. She cleared her throat. "I wondered if you'd like to come over tonight. To my house."

"Huh?" The invitation took Reva by surprise.

"We're trimming the tree tonight. I thought maybe you'd like to come help."

"Well . . . is Victor coming?" Reva asked.

Pam shook her head, the ponytail wagging behind her. "He can't make it. He has to go somewhere with his parents."

"Well, yeah," Reva said. "I'll come. It'll be fun."

I feel guilty, I guess, Reva realized. That's why I'm agreeing to go over to Pam's and be bored out of my mind.

"We'll have popcorn and egg nog and a fire and everything," Pam gushed, squeezing Reva's hand. "It'll be like an old-fashioned Christmas."

"Great!" Reva replied, trying to imitate her cousin's enthusiasm. "Great, Pam!"

A little after seven-thirty that evening, Reva pulled her car onto Fear Street and headed toward Pam's house. The rain had finally stopped that afternoon, but the road was still wet and slick. The old trees that bent over the street on both sides glistened in the pale streetlights.

As she drove past the burned-out Simon Fear mansion, which overlooked the Fear Street Cemetery, Reva shook her head scornfully. How can Pam live on such a creepy, rundown street? she wondered. Surely, Uncle Bill could find a better house, even on his pitiful salary.

Pam's rambling old house came into view. To Reva's surprise, the porch light wasn't on. Probably broken, she thought, like everything else in Pam's house.

She pulled the Miata up the gravel driveway, stopping at the cracked and rutted flagstone walk that led to the front stoop.

She grabbed the shopping bag on the passenger seat. It contained the presents she had bought for Pam and her parents. As Reva climbed out of the car, Pam appeared on the front porch.

"Right on time! Hi!" Pam called cheerily, waving as Reva started to make her way along the front walk. "Hey—you weren't supposed to bring presents tonight!"

"Just a few things to put under your tree," Reva called.

She slipped, turning her ankle on a crack in the walk. "Ow."

"Be careful. The flagstones are all loose," Pam said, stepping down.

Out of the corner of her eye Reva saw something move from around the side of the house.

A darting shadow.

She heard a scraping sound. Hard breathing.

Before she could turn to see what it was, a gloved hand clamped hard over her mouth.

The shopping bag dropped from Reva's hand.

Something heavy was pulled over her head. Something wool and scratchy.

A blanket?

"Hey—I can't see!" she cried, her voice muffled under the weight of the blanket.

An arm swept around her waist, grabbed her tightly.

"Stop!" she heard Pam shriek. "Hey—help! Help!"

With a choked gasp Pam's cries were cut off.

Reva thrashed her elbows back hard.

"Ow!" Her attacker cried out as an elbow made contact. "My mouth!"

Reva felt his arm slip away.

This is my chance, she thought, gripped with panic.

She tried to squirm out from under the blanket.

But her attacker recovered quickly. He wrapped his arm tightly over the blanket, around her throat, tightening, tightening.

Choking off her air.

Then a hard shove from behind sent her sprawling forward.

"You'll pay," he whispered coldly. "You'll pay."

Another hard shove. She realized she was being pushed down the driveway.

This isn't happening, Reva thought, overcome with terror.

This isn't happening.

"Help! Pam—help!" she cried.

Reva struggled and pulled up a corner of the heavy blanket.

She got a quick glimpse of Pam. Pam had been taken too.

But before the blanket was jammed back over her head, Reva got a quick glimpse of the car they were being dragged toward.

A beat-up old Plymouth.

Chapter 26

BODY BAGS IN THE TRASH DUMP

Before Reva saw her attackers, the wool blanket was pulled back over her head, blinding her, choking her.

She cried out as someone again shoved her hard from behind.

"What do you want? Leave us alone!" she heard Pam scream, her voice shrill.

"Shut up!" a girl snapped in a loud, raspy whisper. "Just shut up—both of you."

Reva stumbled, but a strong arm grabbed her around the waist and kept her moving.

She heard a car door open. "Put them both in back," she heard the girl order.

How many were there? Reva wondered.

"What are you going to do to us?" Pam cried.

"I *told* you to *shut up!*" the girl cried furiously.

Reva heard a hard *thud.* Pam cried out in pain.

"Get them in the car. I'll drive," the girl said.

"I'll drive. I've got the keys." A man's voice. No. A teenager's voice.

"Just *move!*" the girl shouted angrily.

"Get in there!" Another man's voice. The man holding Reva. He shoved her. She stumbled forward, thrusting her arms out to break her fall.

She landed on a car seat. She fell into the car, tangled in the blanket. Her knee bumped the car floor.

She could hear Pam struggling behind her. Another *thud,* the sound of a fist landing a hard blow.

"Move!"

"Let us go! You can't get away with this!" Reva heard Pam cry.

And then Pam was shoved in next to her. Reva could feel her trembling body.

Reva heard Pam sob. "Not again! Please—not again! Let me go!"

Then there was a flurry of movement.

Someone opened the car door next to Reva. Someone pulled the blanket off her head. Reva got a glimpse of a pudgy-faced, dark-eyed man in a denim jacket.

A glimpse. Then everything was dark again as a scarf was tied around her eyes.

She wanted to resist, to fight, to make it tough for them. But there was no room to struggle. And her fear made her muscles weak. She could barely raise her arms.

Reva's hands were pulled roughly behind her back. Then they were tied with some kind of cord. "Ow—no!" She cried out as the cord cut into her wrists.

Her cry was ignored.

The car door slammed shut.

She could still feel Pam's trembling body beside her.

"Reva—are you okay?" Pam whispered.

"Shut up! Shut *up!*" the girl rasped from the driver's seat. "Hurry up, Pres!"

"Hey—no names!" the boy shouted angrily.

Pres? One of them was named Pres?

Reva figured there were three of them. The woman, the pudgy-faced man who had pushed her into the car, and the teenage boy. The one named Pres.

She heard a front door slam.

The car engine roared. The car shot forward, throwing Reva back against the seat.

"Sit back and enjoy the ride," the man said. Reva could tell he was sitting next to Pam.

"You *can't* do this!" Pam cried in a weak, trembling voice.

Reva remained silent. Staring into the blackness behind the blindfold. She realized she was too frightened to speak.

She coughed. Started to choke. Her throat felt tight and dry.

"Stop coughing, Reva!" the girl snapped from the front seat.

She knows my name, Reva thought. A cold chill ran down her back.

They know my name. They've planned this. They've been sitting somewhere, planning this, talking about me.

Reva had read about kidnappings. She had seen movies about them on TV.

But the movies never showed the real fear, she thought, feeling her whole body convulse in a shudder.

The movies never showed the darkness. Never showed the panic that choked you, that made you gasp, that made your temples throb.

The movies never showed the horror of being helpless, of being at the mercy of someone who wanted to harm you.

To hurt you. To kill you, maybe.

Someone who knew your name . . .

This is what Pam went through, Reva realized. This is the fear Pam felt.

And now it is happening all over again to her.

Why? Because of me?

If they wanted to kidnap me, why did they take Pam again?

The answer came to Reva at once. *They think they can get more money if they have both of us.*

They're probably right, Reva realized.

Daddy will gladly pay them whatever they want.

And then what?

The question flashed uninvited into her mind.

And then what?

Reva didn't want to think about that question.

What will they do to Pam and me once Daddy has paid them? Will they return us to our homes? Will they simply dump us out on my driveway the way they did the first time?

Reva had seen the movies. She'd seen the news stories on TV about kidnappings.

Sometimes they let you go home. Sometimes they took the money and let you go.

But sometimes they didn't. Sometimes they . . . killed you.

Killed you and hid your body where the police wouldn't find it until it was rotted.

Took the money and killed you anyway. And dropped your body in a river or in some filthy trash dump. And then when they showed you on TV, you were zipped into one of those long plastic body bags. Wrapped up like garbage. And—and—

Stop! Reva ordered herself. Stop thinking such horrible things!

You'll be okay. Daddy will pay. They'll let you go.

Think positive.

They already let Pam go once—right?

The car squealed as it made a hard turn around a corner. Then it shot forward with a roar.

Reva realized she'd been holding her breath. She let it out slowly, trying to stop her body from trembling, trying to keep the frightening thoughts, the ugly pictures, from invading her mind.

"Merry Christmas to us!" the boy in the front

seat exclaimed suddenly. He let out a high-pitched, gleeful cheer.

"Whoa. Don't start celebrating now," the girl replied from the driver's seat. "We don't have the money yet, remember?"

The boy let out another cheer. "Merry Christmas, one and all!"

The car turned another corner. Reva felt Pam thrown against her.

"Hey, you're being awful quiet," the boy called back to the man squeezed on the other side of Pam.

"I got hit in the mouth," the man muttered glumly.

"Who hit you?" the boy asked.

"The redhead. You know. Reva," the man rasped angrily. "She got me with her elbow when I was taking her to the car."

Reva heard the boy snicker.

"It isn't funny, Pres," the man snapped furiously, forgetting about not using names. "She split my lip. It's bleeding like crazy."

Good, Reva thought.

"It brought my headache back," the man grumbled. "Real bad."

"You'll be okay," the girl said without any sympathy. "You won't have your headaches when you're rich. I'll make you a bet."

"I just want to kill her," the man fumed, ignoring the girl's words.

"Hey, come on, man. Sit back and relax," Pres said. "We're almost there."

"I want to kill her. I really do," the man insisted calmly. His words were slightly slurred. Reva guessed it was because of the split lip she had given him.

"Well . . . maybe you'll get your chance," the boy replied casually.

Chapter 27

QUIET AS DEATH

"I want to break her arm in thirty places," the man in the backseat said, breathing noisily, excitedly. "Then maybe my headache will go away."

"Hey, we have a lot to do. We have to keep control, remember?" the girl called back to him, sounding very impatient.

The man grumbled a reply.

The car slowed to a stop.

"Where are you taking us?" Reva blurted out. "What are you going to do?"

"Hey, it speaks," the girl said sarcastically.

"We told you to shut up!" the man growled at Reva.

"This cord is cutting my wrist," Reva complained.

"Boo-hoo," the girl replied coldly. "You'd better shut your trap, Reva."

"I just want to know what you're planning to do," Reva insisted.

"Say one more word and it's all over," the girl told her flatly.

Pam bumped Reva hard, signaling for her not to say any more. Reva choked back her questions and sank into the seat.

"Pull the car back there," she heard Pres instruct the girl.

"You checked this all out?" the girl asked him skeptically.

"Yeah. As soon as I got back," Pres told her. "There's no guard back here. You'll see. Park it over there. Away from the lights."

The car lurched forward.

Pam leaned hard against Reva. She had stopped trembling, but Reva could hear her frightened, shallow breaths.

"No mess-ups this time," the man beside Pam muttered.

"Hey, no way. I'm back now," Pres said lightly. "What could go wrong?"

The car slowed to a halt. Reva heard the girl shift into Park, then turn the engine off. "Less talk, more action," she muttered.

"Aye, aye, captain," the man replied sarcastically.

"Pull them out," the girl instructed.

Car doors opened. Reva heard the kidnappers climb out.

"Where are we?" Reva whispered to Pam.

"I don't know," Pam whispered back. "It seems like we've been driving for a long time. But I think it's just because I'm so scared."

"Shut up! Both of you!" the man snarled. "You're giving me a headache."

He yanked Reva out of the car. She stumbled, then caught her balance. Her shoes scraped against hard pavement.

A driveway? she wondered. Some kind of parking lot?

So this is what it's like to be blind, she suddenly realized.

The air felt cold and refreshing on her face. She took a deep breath, then another.

If only her heart would stop racing, thudding so hard in her chest.

She could hear Pam being pulled from the car. Then car doors slammed.

Reva listened hard.

Where are we? Where?

It was so quiet. Quiet as death.

She shivered.

Someone shoved her hands up roughly against her back. She cried out as the tight cords dug into her skin.

The man shoved her arms up again. The pain shot through her entire body. Then he pushed her forward. "Which door?" he called to the others.

"That one," Reva heard Pres reply. "With the light burned out."

Reva could hear Pam close beside her. They were both being pushed up steps.

Where are we? Where are we? Where are we? The question repeated in Reva's mind.

She could hear traffic muffled in the distance. The sound of a car honking, far away. The only other sound was the scraping of their shoes on the hard pavement.

"Oh!" Reva suddenly stumbled and fell. With her hands tied behind her, she couldn't break her fall. She landed hard on her side. Pain shot up her back. "Ohh."

"Don't pull any funny business," the man growled angrily.

"I can't see!" Reva wailed.

He grabbed her around the waist and hoisted her to her feet. "There's nothing to see," he said. "Just walk."

Reva's knee ached. She uttered a low sob. "Help me!"

The man laughed scornfully.

"Hurry up. Someone will see us," the girl cried sharply.

The man shoved Reva forward. "You heard the lady. Move it."

A second later they had gone through a door and were walking across a silent room. From the way their footsteps echoed, Reva could tell it was a large room.

She coughed loudly. The cough echoed all around.

A very large room.

The floor was hard. She scraped her sneakers as she walked. Not smooth. Not linoleum or tile. Concrete, maybe.

Into another room.

"Stay to your right against the wall," Reva heard the girl urge.

Reva took a deep breath. They were walking quickly. The man had her arm, squeezing it painfully, pushing her forward.

Reva took another deep breath, trying to remain in control, trying not to fall apart.

She realized what she was smelling.

I know where we are, she thought.

I know where we are. And I don't believe it!

Chapter 28

REVA GETS A BREAK

Reva recognized the heavy warmth of the air, the tangy sweet aroma of the perfume and cosmetics.

Someone had left the sound system on, very low. She could hear a chorus, very soft, singing "Silent Night."

We're in Daddy's store, Reva realized, astonished.

They've brought Pam and me to the department store.

But why?

"Pres, where'd you go?" the man asked suddenly.

"Hey—no names, remember?" Pres snapped. "I had to knock out the security guard. Let's hurry upstairs."

"See if they left the elevators running," the man said. "I really don't feel like walking up five floors."

"Hey, she gave you a nasty cut on your lip," Pres exclaimed. "You should put some ice on that."

"Good idea. Let's send out for ice," the girl said sarcastically. "Maybe we'll order some sandwiches while we're at it."

"Okay, okay. Lighten up," Pres told her. "Everything's going great—for once. We're going to be rich. Millionaires. Just like in the movies."

"You and your brother are both alike," the girl muttered. "Counting your chickens before they're hatched."

"Cluck-cluck," Pres replied.

"Hey, the elevator!" the man cried. "Good deal." He pulled Reva's arm. "Get in."

Reva was shoved up against the back of the elevator. She could feel Pam right beside her. The elevator emitted a low hum as it began to rise.

Why are they taking us to the fifth floor? Reva asked herself. What's on the fifth floor?

Children's clothes. And toys, she remembered. Yes. Santa's World is up there this year. And a children's hair salon. An inexpensive shoe boutique . . .

Why the fifth floor?

"This way," the man said, jerking her roughly out of the elevator.

"I know where we are," Reva blurted out. "My father's store."

"Well, you win the prize," the girl replied sarcastically. "Pull off their blindfolds. Otherwise we'll never get them to the room."

Reva had to shut her eyes against the invasion of bright light. Blinking, she waited for them to adjust. She saw Pam squinting against the sudden light too.

As they continued to walk through a narrow back hallway, the three kidnappers came into clear focus. The woman was young, Reva saw, probably not even twenty. She had a bad bleach job, her dark roots showing. She'd be nice looking if it weren't for the buck teeth, Reva observed.

And then she remembered them.

From the store a few mornings before. The dropped contact lens. The younger guy, Pres, the one with the soulful black eyes and thin, wasted look—he had tried to pull her away from the counter.

Yes, Reva remembered them both. The third one, the pudgy one with the beer belly and the red face, she'd never seen before. His eyes were darting wildly around. His lip was swollen on one side, dried blood clinging to the spot that was cut.

Pres was kind of good-looking in a cheap, trashy way, Reva thought. He sneered at Reva, sizing her up as if seeing her for the first time.

She turned her glance to Pam. Pam's blond hair was disheveled. Her eyes were red-rimmed and bloodshot. She tried to flash Reva an encouraging smile, but her quivering chin gave her away, revealing her fear.

"Move it. Hurry!" the girl urged with a scowl. "There's a security guard somewhere on this floor."

Reva and Pam were forced along the narrow passageway behind the selling floor. Doorways led to supply closets and storage rooms.

"In there," the man barked, shoving Reva's shoulder.

A glint of light caught Reva's eye. She gasped as she realized for the first time that he was carrying a small silver pistol in one hand.

"Yeah. It's real," he growled, narrowing his eyes at her. "Just give me a reason to use it. Go ahead, Reva."

The way he pronounced her name made it sound like a curse word.

Where are the cleaning people? Where are the night guards? Reva wondered. She knew the TV surveillance system was broken and being repaired. She realized that the kidnappers must have scoped out the store and known this, must have known also that the cleaners were finished on the fifth floor by this time every night.

She and Pam were shoved into a small square storage room. Metal shelves against the back wall were empty. A short aluminum ladder stood in front of the shelves. Two gray folding chairs had been placed in the center of the room.

The floor and chairs were covered with dust. Empty soda cans were strewn on the floor around the two chairs.

Some workers probably eat their lunch in here, Reva observed. But it's pretty obvious this storage room hasn't been used in some time.

The girl motioned for Pam and Reva to go to the two folding chairs.

"Can't you untie my hands?" Reva demanded shrilly. "The cord—it's cutting my skin."

The girl *tsk-tsk*ed sarcastically.

"Can't you just *loosen* them a little?" Reva pleaded. "Can't you give me a break? You're going to take money from my father, right? So can't you treat me with a little respect, a little dignity, maybe?"

"Enough! That's enough!" the man cried angrily. He had been fingering his cut lip. Now his eyes widened in anger. His face reddened as he strode toward Reva.

"Danny—" the girl called warily, accidentally revealing the man's name to Reva and Pam.

"Whoa, man," Pres urged.

Ignoring his two partners, Danny grabbed Reva's arm.

"Let *go* of me!" she screamed.

He pulled the arm up behind her.

"Danny—let go," the girl ordered.

"Please—let go! You're really *hurting* me!" Reva pleaded in a shrill, frightened voice she'd never heard before. *"Please!"*

"Danny—*don't!"* the girl shouted.

But with an angry grunt Danny jerked Reva's arm up hard.

The loud *crack* sounded like a pencil snapping.

The pain flared up Reva's arm, up her back, her neck. Everything turned white. The floor tilted up toward her.

The pain sizzled like an electric current, surging over her, surrounding her, pulling her down.

Breathing hard, Danny let go and stepped back.

Silently Reva dropped to her knees on the glaring white floor, the white walls shimmering in front of her.

Were those low moans coming from *her?*

She couldn't hear herself over the deafening roar of pain.

The white pain. The white, sizzling pain.

With another low moan Reva shut her eyes.

It was white inside her eyelids. Blinding white.

The roar grew louder.

And over the roar she heard Danny say, "I really want to kill her."

Chapter 29

ONE MORE SURPRISE FOR REVA

Reva realized she must have blacked out.

Blinking her eyes, she glanced around. She was sitting now. Beside Pam. In one of the two folding chairs. A steady throb of pain shot up her arm.

She tried to stand up. Then realized she was tied at the waist. Tied to the chair. Her hands still tied behind her.

The angry white glare had disappeared. Everything seemed in soft focus now, slightly blurred.

Tied up beside her, Pam mouthed the words, *Are you okay?*

Reva furrowed her forehead. She tried to shrug, but the pain was too great.

Okay? Am I okay?

The question didn't make any sense to her. No sense at all.

How could I be okay?

Struggling to focus, she gazed around the room.

Danny hovered by the door, glancing out nervously.

The girl and Pres stood against the wall, staring back at Reva. "She's coming to," Pres murmured.

"I've got eyes," the girl replied sharply.

"I told you we shouldn't get Danny involved," Pres said, eyeing his brother. "He's out of control. He could do *anything.*"

Reva shuddered.

He could do anything?

He's already broken my arm, she thought, feeling the heavy dread form like a rock in her stomach. What else is he going to do to me?

Are they really going to let him kill me?

"I said I was sorry," Danny told Pres, his eyes still trained on the door. "How many times do I have to apologize? I just lost it for a moment, that's all. I feel better now. I really do. So give me a break, Diane."

The girl rolled her eyes. "Thanks for telling them my name," she said. "Can we stick to our plan now? Now that you've had your fun?"

"Yeah. Fine," Danny muttered.

Diane stepped over to Reva. "You okay?"

Reva glared at her and didn't reply.

Diane pulled up a strand of Reva's hair. She lowered her gaze to examine it. Then she let it drop with a sneer on her face.

"Go find a phone," Pres said. "This place is giving me the creeps."

"I don't get it. Why did you bring us here, to Daddy's store?" Reva demanded, wincing from the pain in her broken arm.

"It's the *last* place anyone would look," Diane told her, walking to the door.

"No one uses these storage rooms," Pres confided. "No one ever comes back here. I checked it all out." He seemed really pleased with himself.

"So go call Dalby," Danny urged Diane. "Tell him where to drop the money."

"Yeah. Then we can get out of here," Pres agreed.

"But what about us?" Reva asked. She glanced beside her at Pam. Pam was staring intently at Pres, as if memorizing every pore of his face. "What are you going to do with us?" Reva repeated.

"Leave you tied up here," Diane replied without any expression. "And gagged."

"But—but—" Reva stammered.

"Don't sweat it," Diane said, frowning. "Someone will find you in a day or two."

Pres snickered. He motioned for Diane to go make her call.

"I still think we should kill them," Danny said, waving the small pistol.

"Danny, we've been over and over that," Diane sighed. "You've had your fun, okay? You broke her arm. Now listen to me. We just want to make some Christmas money, remember? We don't want to kill them." She uttered an exasperated sigh.

"But why leave witnesses?" Danny demanded.

"They've seen us, Diane. They know our names. If we don't kill them, they'll help the police. We'll be caught."

"No way," Pres assured his brother. "We'll be so far away from here, it won't matter. Besides, I told you. No one ever comes back to this storage area. These girls could be here for a week. Longer."

Danny rubbed his forehead with his free hand. "I guess I'm not thinking clearly. I mean, I always remember the old saying, you know? *Dead men tell no tales.*"

"Danny, this isn't a pirate movie," Diane said sharply, shaking her head. "It's a kidnapping movie."

Was that just a slip? Or does she really think she's in a movie? Reva wondered. Does she really think it's all pretend or something?

They're crazy! Reva exclaimed to herself. All three of them. They're all crazy.

She stared hard at the pistol gripped in Danny's pudgy hand.

Crazy and dangerous.

"I'm going down the hall to call Dalby," Diane announced, ending the conversation. "Then we'll get out of here. Pres, double-check the cords. Make sure they're tied really tight. We'll gag them when we're ready to leave."

She started to the door, taking long, hurried strides.

"Wait a minute!" Pam called.

Her cry startled Reva. Pam hadn't uttered a sound all this time.

"Wait a minute, Diane," Pam called. "Let me go now. Untie me."

Diane turned at the doorway and locked her eyes on Pam. "No way," she said coldly.

"Hey, you promised!" Pam cried shrilly. "Let me go. Come on, Diane. You promised. You promised if I got you Reva, you'd let me go!"

Chapter 30

PAM'S DEAL

"Huh?" Reva gasped in shock. She struggled to turn toward Pam, but the effort sent a lightning bolt of pain up her arm. She narrowed her eyes at her cousin. "You—you made a *deal* with them?" Her voice revealed more shock than anger. Shock and hurt.

Pam avoided Reva's eyes. "Sure. Why not?" she muttered. "Hey—Diane—wait!" she called desperately.

Ignoring her, Diane disappeared to make her call.

"Come on, you guys! Let me go. You promised!" Pam wailed.

Pres and Danny ignored Pam too. They huddled in the corner, talking rapidly in low tones. Pres had a hand on Danny's shoulder. Danny was still gripping the silver pistol in one hand.

"You *helped* them?" Reva cried in disbelief, her voice a shrill whisper. "How *could* you, Pam? How could you?"

"Easy," Pam replied, turning to Reva with a sneer on her face. "Why do you think they let me go?"

"Because you—you—" Reva was so shocked and upset, she could barely speak.

Pam's eyes burned into Reva's. "You broke my heart, Reva," she said bitterly.

"Huh? I *what?"* Reva felt the room tilt again. "I don't understand, Pam. You're my cousin. I can't believe you'd agree to—"

"You knew I was in love with Victor," Pam said, her green eyes flaring, her features tight with anger.

"Huh? Victor? But—"

"You knew I was in love with Victor," Pam repeated through clenched teeth. "And you didn't care. You went out with him anyway. You sneaked out with him. You knew how much I cared, and you sneaked out. You tried to steal him. You—"

"What are you talking about?" Reva asked, careful not to meet her cousin's eye.

"Don't lie to me," Pam warned. "I know about you and Victor. The minute you said he broke two dates with me, I knew. I told you about only one of those dates. You knew because *you* were the one out with Victor!"

"But, Pam, it wasn't anything serious!" Reva protested.

"That's even *worse!"* Pam cried.

"Hey—keep it down over there," Danny ordered from the corner, glaring at them. "You want me to put the gags on now?"

"That's even worse," Pam repeated to Reva in a whisper.

"But, Pam—"

"You did that to me, and it was just some kind of joke to you?" Pam whispered shrilly. "Just some kind of casual joke? That's worse, Reva. Much worse."

Reva winced in pain. Her arm was throbbing more. The pain tightened the back of her neck. She was having trouble focusing her eyes.

"Why did you do it, Reva?" Pam demanded. "Why? Why did you want to hurt me like that?"

"I—I don't know," Reva whispered.

I really *don't* know, Reva thought. I don't know why I was so eager to steal Victor. It was just a game, that's all. I really wasn't interested in him. I didn't even like him very much.

"When I found out," Pam whispered, raising her eyes to Pres and Danny, who were still huddled against the wall, "when I found out about you and Victor, I wanted to kill you, Reva. I really did."

"I'm . . . sorry," Reva replied, lowering her eyes.

"Then I was kidnapped. Because of you. Because you practically *forced* me to take your shift in the stockroom. The kidnappers never wanted me. They wanted you, of course."

"I know," Reva replied, shutting her eyes. "I know."

"Then your father refused to pay any ransom money for me," Pam continued bitterly. "Uncle Robert wouldn't pay a dime for me. He had his precious Reva home safe and sound. Why should he pay anything for me, a lowly niece?"

"Pam, really—" Reva tried to interrupt.

But Pam was determined to have her say. "When your father refused to pay, that's when I realized I had nothing to lose. I . . . I was so hurt, Reva. And so angry. And I didn't want to die. So I made a deal with them."

"They offered you *money?"* Reva asked.

Pam glared at her scornfully. "Money? That's all you can think about, isn't it, Reva. Money and other people's boyfriends." She scowled. "No. They didn't offer me money. They didn't have to."

"You mean—" Reva started.

"They offered to let me go. They offered to let me go home safe and sound—if I agreed to help them grab you. And I thought, why shouldn't I? Why shouldn't I think of *myself* for a change?"

"But, Pam," Reva said in a trembling voice, "I'm your cousin. I'm your family. How could you—"

"How could *you?"* Pam snapped back furiously. "Besides, I knew nothing bad would happen. So Uncle Robert will have to lose a million or two. Big deal. That doesn't mean anything to him. And you—you'll be home in time for Christmas in front of the tree and all the hundreds of presents your father showers you with every year."

"Yeah. I'll be home. With a broken arm," Reva muttered.

Pam glared at her but didn't reply. "You don't care about me, so why should I care about you?" she said finally.

"But you—you *betrayed* me!" Reva cried.

"No. You betrayed me," Pam replied sadly. Tears brimmed in her eyes. "You betrayed me, Reva. You promised last year that you were going to change. You promised we'd be like sisters. You promised—" Her voice broke. She uttered an angry sob.

"I tried," Reva said softly. "It's hard to change, Pam. It's hard to—"

"I don't want to hear about it," Pam snapped. A tear ran down each pale cheek. She raised her head to Pres and Danny. "Untie me," she shouted. "Come on. Untie me."

The two brothers turned to stare at her, but neither replied.

"I'm going home now," Pam insisted, straining at the cords that held her to the folding chair. "I delivered my cousin. Now, let me go. We have a deal."

Danny shook his head. Pres snickered. "You should've gotten it in writing," he said with an amused sneer.

"Let me go!" Pam shouted angrily. "Let me go!"

"Hey—shut up!" Danny ordered, taking a few steps toward the two girls.

"No! Let me go! Let me go!" Pam screamed. "I'm going to shout till you do it! Let me go!"

"She'll bring a guard!" Pres warned his brother, panic creeping into his dark eyes.

Danny moved with surprising speed.

"Let me go! Let me go!" Pam chanted at the top of her lungs.

With an angry groan Danny pulled his hand back—and swung it hard, slapping Pam across the face.

The slap was so hard, it sounded like a gunshot.

Pam's head snapped back.

The chair tilted and nearly toppled over.

Danny leaned over her, breathing hard, his big stomach heaving up and down.

Pam's eyes were open wide. Her head rolled on her shoulders.

She didn't utter a sound.

"Pam!" Reva cried in fear. "Pam!"

A gurgling sound escaped from Pam.

Then her eyes closed and her head slumped forward lifelessly.

Chapter 31

NO ESCAPE

Reva saw Pres freeze by the door. Danny continued to lean over Pam, breathing heavily through his open mouth.

"Hey. Sit up," Danny ordered Pam. He turned back to Pres. "I didn't hit her that hard."

"You did too!" Reva insisted. She couldn't get the loud snap out of her mind. Again she saw Danny's backhanded slap, saw the chair nearly tilt over backward, saw Pam's head fly back.

Snap.

"Sit up," Danny repeated angrily.

Pam groaned. Slowly she raised her head.

Reva breathed a loud sigh of relief. "Pam—you're okay?"

Pam nodded groggily. She had a bright red circle on her cheek, the spot where the slap had landed.

"I knew I didn't hit her that hard," Danny told Pres, beads of perspiration glistening on his wide forehead. "I just knocked her breath out."

Pres started to reply, but Diane burst back into the room. "What's going on in here?" she demanded, eyeing Reva and Pam.

"Not much," Pres replied quickly.

"Pretty quiet," Danny said.

"How'd it go? Did you reach Dalby?" Pres asked.

The smile on Diane's face indicated that she had. She threw her arms around Pres and gave him a jubilant hug. "We're going to be rich, honey!" They kissed.

"Did you tell him the drop-off?" Danny demanded excitedly. "When's he getting us the money?"

Diane turned away from Pres. Her smile faded. "Not in front of them," she said, gesturing at the two girls. "Come on. Let's talk outside."

They turned off the single bulb, leaving Reva and Pam in darkness. Then Pres and Danny followed Diane out into the hall. The storage-room door closed behind them. Reva heard them walk a short way down the hall.

"I'm sorry, Reva," Pam said in a tiny voice. She was still groggy, Reva realized.

"I'm really sorry," Pam repeated.

"I'm sorry too," Reva replied sincerely.

"I was so stupid," Pam said, tears rolling down her cheeks. "How could I have believed them? How could I have trusted them?"

"You were angry," Reva said softly. "And desperate. They might have killed you."

"Now what?" Pam whispered.

Reva swallowed hard. Her throat felt dry as cotton. "I don't know." She groaned in pain. "My arm—it's completely numb. But it still hurts every time I move."

"We have to get out of here," Pam muttered, gazing toward the closed door.

"Huh?" Reva stared through the darkness at her.

"They're crazy," Pam said. "Danny especially. They say they're just going to leave us here. They say they're not going to harm us. But—"

"You think—?" Reva started.

"You heard Danny," Pam continued, her voice trembling. "He wants to kill us. We've seen them. We know their names. Danny doesn't want any witnesses."

"I can hear him out in the hall," Reva said, feeling a tremor of fear.

"He's arguing with them," Pam said, listening too. "Probably trying to convince Pres and Diane. To—to kill us."

"Maybe he won't win the argument," Reva said.

"Maybe he will," Pam replied grimly. "Reva, we have to get out of here."

Reva let out a hopeless sigh. "Get out of here? How? Do you know any magic words?"

"I'm not tied very tightly," Pam revealed. "I think Pres went easy on me because I was cooperating with them. Or maybe he just messed up."

Her shoulders rolled up and down as she began to work her hands behind the chair. "The cord's very loose," she said, trying to tug herself free.

"You really think you can untie it?" Reva asked.

Pam nodded. "I . . . think . . . so. . . ."

"But even if we get untied—then what?" Reva demanded, panic slipping into her voice.

"I guess we make a run for it," Pam said. "Maybe we can surprise them. You know, catch them off guard."

"Run right past them?" Reva asked, staring at the closed door.

"It's worth a try," Pam murmured darkly.

"I guess," Reva replied. "There's *got* to be a security guard on this floor. Maybe we can find him before—"

Pam interrupted with a frustrated cry. "This is taking longer than I thought." She continued to struggle, leaning forward, then leaning back, her shoulders moving as her hands worked behind her.

"Hurry," Reva urged. She could hear Danny and the others still arguing out in the hall.

"Almost got it," Pam said, breathing hard.

"This is the fifth floor. I know this floor pretty well," Reva told her. "We must be right behind Santa's World. There are a lot of tall shelves of toys. Lots of places to hide."

"Yes!" Pam whispered triumphantly. She swung her hands in front of her and tossed away the loosened cord. Then she began working furiously at the cord around her waist, the cord that held her to the chair.

A few seconds later she tossed that cord aside too. Climbing to her feet, she stretched her arms over her head. "Ooh, I'm so stiff."

"Hurry. Untie me," Reva urged. "It got very quiet out in the hall. They'll be back any second."

"Hope you can run," Pam whispered, her hands tugging frantically at a knot in the cord that held Reva's hands. "I mean, I hope the pain isn't too bad. From your arm."

"I can run," Reva assured her, eyes on the storage-room door.

Working frantically in the dark, Pam tugged away Reva's cords. Reva climbed quickly to her feet. She cried out from a stab of pain in her arm, then quickly covered her mouth to stifle the sound.

The two girls stood awkwardly in the center of the room.

"Now what?" Reva whispered.

Pam's swollen cheek blazed. Her eyes widened in fear. "I—I don't know. I guess we should hide against the wall beside the door. When they come in, maybe they'll walk right past us—and we can make a run for it."

"Good!" Reva cried, her heart thudding in her chest. Each heartbeat seemed to send a throbbing wave of pain up from her broken arm. The arm hung lifelessly at her left side. She bit down hard on her lower lip, trying to force away the pain.

Both girls started toward the wall—but stopped short when the door was opened.

"I'll take care of them," they heard Pres say.

We're caught, Reva realized, frozen in helpless horror.

Chapter 32

FALLING BODIES

The door was standing halfway open. A pale triangle of light slanted into the room.

Reva stared open-mouthed, standing awkwardly, swallowing hard. Pam stood just ahead of her, also frozen in fear.

"I *said* I'll take care of them," Pres called irritably to his two partners.

Take care of them. What did that mean? Reva wondered.

She heard Diane's voice out in the hall. She was asking Pres something.

"Okay," he muttered.

The door was pushed shut.

He didn't come in.

Reva gaped at Pam. Giddy laughter escaped her throat. "We're safe."

"For now," Pam said, sobering quickly.

Reva crept along the wall, stopping just short of the doorway. Pam followed right behind.

"As soon as the door opens again, we run out," Reva whispered, cringing in pain. She had leaned against the wall with her broken arm, and the pain roared out like a raging fire.

Pam nodded solemnly, listening to the conversation between the three kidnappers on the other side of the wall. "Which way do we run?"

"Right," Reva whispered. "Toward Santa's World. And scream as loud as you can. Maybe we can wake up the guard."

Pam touched the swollen welt on her cheek. "Shhhh. They're coming."

She took a deep breath.

The walls seemed to shimmer and shake for Reva. The whole room grew brighter, glowing until she had to shut her eyes. The floor tilted first one way, then the other.

Don't freak, Reva, she scolded herself. You'll never get away if you totally lose it.

She heard footsteps in the hall.

The door started to open.

This is it, she thought.

Pres entered the room. He took several steps, staring straight ahead at the two empty folding chairs.

Reva just had time to see his mouth drop open in shock. She heard his astonished gasp.

Then she and Pam took off.

Out the door. Into the narrow passageway.

"Hey—" Danny's startled cry echoed in the hallway. He and Diane were against the wall several yards away. They seemed to freeze, startled by the unexpected sight of the two girls fleeing.

Reva's sneakers squeaked over the hard linoleum floor. Her broken arm flopped painfully against her side. She kept her good arm stretched out in front of her, as if poised to stiff-arm tacklers.

"Help!" she screamed. *"Hellllp!"*

Pain cut through her body as she ran. Turned right. Hurtled herself past dark, empty storage rooms.

She could hear Pam right behind her.

"Hey—stop!" Danny's angry shout.

She turned her head without slowing her pace. Danny and Diane were close behind, Pres a few yards behind them.

"Ow!" she cried out as she collided with a large metal trash basket. "Oh!" She spun off it. The trash can rolled noisily back into her pursuers.

Reva lurched onto the selling floor.

So bright. Christmas decorations sparkling in the night light. Gold and silver tinsel everywhere. Shimmering Christmas balls.

Like a fairyland, she thought.

Only this is no fairy tale.

"Help! Help us—please!"

"They're going to catch us!" Pam shrieked breathlessly.

"Split up!" Reva cried. "Split up! Go!"

She saw Pam turn, stumble, quickly regain her balance, and push herself off a display case of children's boots. Reva kept going, running straight, gasping noisily for breath, her chest about to explode.

She turned. Then turned again. She ducked low, turning and twisting through the maze of display counters and aisles.

She couldn't see her pursuers. Had she lost them?

Into Santa's World. All red and green, silver and gold. Past the enormous wooden sleigh. Past the reindeers staring glassy-eyed at her as she ran. Past the elves lined up as if waiting for Santa to ascend his gold throne.

"Help! Please—help!" Reva tried to scream, but her voice came out a hushed whisper.

Where was the stupid security guard? Maybe there *wasn't* one on this floor. Maybe that's why the kidnappers chose this floor.

I can't run much farther, Reva realized.

She reached a wall, a dead end. With a gasp she took a step back. Then another.

Which way? Which way?

A hand touched her back.

"No!"

She spun around.

Santa Claus grinned at her.

She had backed into a Santa mannequin.

Just like in my dream, she thought, gasping for breath.

She started to run again. Around a display of children's sweaters. Into the toy department.

"Where did she go?" Danny's voice, in a distant aisle, sounded confused as he chased after Pam.

Maybe Pam is getting away, Reva thought.

She bumped an enormous lifesize Ninja Turtle stuffed animal that guarded an aisle in silent menace. Its head bounced angrily.

She glanced back. And saw Pres behind her, his dark eyes burning furiously into her back.

Diane and Danny must have gone after Pam, Reva figured. Got to lose Pres. But how?

"You can't get away, Reva! There's nowhere to run!" He sounded as breathless as she did. She saw that he was holding his side. He must have had a pain in it from running.

With a powerful heave of her one good arm, Reva shoved the big stuffed animal into his path.

She heard Pres cry out and stumble.

Then she made a sharp left, staying low behind a tall display of Lego blocks, ducked behind a long glass display case of slot cars, and flung herself out into the aisle beyond the toy department.

"Help me! Won't *someone* help me?"

She was hurtling down a long, twisting aisle of budget clothes.

I—I can't breathe, she thought. I can't take another step. I—

She could hear Pres somewhere behind her. She knew she couldn't give up.

With a desperate burst of speed she turned a corner—and ran headlong into someone.

"Oh!"

No. Not someone.

A mannequin. Another mannequin. Not Santa this time.

A wide-eyed woman with bright red hair, dressed in red and blue ski clothes. Reva cried out as pain shot up her shoulder. The mannequin toppled backward onto another mannequin, which fell onto another.

A whole row of mannequins, Reva saw.

All toppling over backward.

Like bodies, she thought, her chest heaving, her temples throbbing.

Like human bodies.

Falling dead, all in a row.

She gaped in breathless horror as the bodies clattered to the floor, landing in a stiff heap of arms and legs, their solid lifeless eyes staring up at the ceiling lights.

And then, before she could start running again, a hand grabbed Reva's shoulder and held on.

Chapter 33

BYE-BYE

Reva spun around. "Pam!"

Pam clung to Reva. She was panting, her chest heaving up and down. Her wet blond hair clung to her forehead. Her green eyes were wide with fear.

"I—I got away from them," she choked out breathlessly. "Where is the guard?"

"There isn't one," Reva replied, her eyes on the aisle behind Pam. "We shouldn't stay here. We have to get downstairs. Come on."

They began creeping side by side, cutting from aisle to aisle, staying low, alert for their pursuers.

Through a dimly lit shoe department. Past a display of running suits and sportswear.

The store seems so much bigger when it's empty, Reva realized. I feel as if I've been going for miles.

Nearly to the back of the store now. She and Pam

glanced at each other as the cries rang out. "This way! Over here!" Reva recognized Pres's angry voice. "Diane—they're over here!"

"They see us!" Pam cried.

Reva began to run. "Keep going," she said, her side aching, her arm throbbing.

The back wall came into view. Is this another dead end? Reva wondered.

No.

The two employee elevators stood just beyond a narrow aisle.

Reva ran to the wall, gasping for breath. She pushed the button. Were the elevators running? Could she and Pam get on them? Could they get away before . . . before—

"No!" Reva cried. She suddenly remembered something. "Pam—this way!"

"Huh?" Pam reacted with surprise, her face red and puffy.

The elevator on the left hummed to life. Pam stared up at the floor indicator above it as the arrow slowly began to move up from the first floor. "It's coming!" Pam whispered. "We have to take it!"

But Reva pulled Pam away. They ducked behind a wide round pillar, pressing their backs against the cool concrete.

"The employee elevators—they're broken again," Reva told Pam, struggling to catch her breath. "I remember. My dad told me they can't figure out why they keep breaking."

"But—but they're *coming!*" Pam whispered, grasping Reva's arm again.

"Maybe we'll get lucky," Reva whispered back,

listening to the approaching footsteps. "Maybe Pres and Diane will think we went down. Maybe they'll try to go after us. You know, jump inside—and fall to the basement."

Pam's face revealed her doubt. "Reva—that's impossible. We can't—"

"Shhhhh!" Reva clamped her hand over Pam's mouth. "Here they come. Be quiet—and pray."

Pressed against the pillar, the two girls watched as Pres and Diane ran up to the elevators, turning their heads to search the aisle. The elevator door on the left slid open.

"This way!" Pres cried, gesturing to the elevator. "They went down. Let's go!"

Reva held her breath and stared hard, afraid to move, afraid to blink.

Both Pres and Diane leapt into the dark elevator at the same time—and dropped to their deaths.

Chapter 34

AN UNWELCOME VISITOR

A low murmur escaped Reva's lips.

She stared into the darkness of the open elevator, afraid to move. Were they gone? Were they really gone?

Had they fallen to their deaths, splattered against the basement floor?

She listened. Silence. A heavy silence.

Then Reva gasped as Pres and Diane stepped back out into the aisle.

They didn't fall. I imagined it, she realized.

I *wished* it.

The employee elevators must have been fixed.

"Let's not panic and act stupid," Diane scolded Pres. "The girls didn't have time to take the elevator down. We were right behind them."

Pres pushed his black hair off his forehead with an angry toss of his head. "Then where are they?" he asked, his face bright red, his dark eyes darting nervously in all directions. "Still on this floor?"

"Yeah," she replied.

"Hey—where'd you guys go?" Danny called from several aisles away.

"Over here, Danny," Pres called back. "Keep looking. They're here somewhere."

"Spread out," Diane urged, hurrying back toward the toy department.

Reva kept her eyes locked on Pres. He lingered for a few seconds, his eyes searching the aisle along the back wall. The elevator door slid shut behind him. He glanced up at the floor indicator as the arrow moved back toward the first floor. Then, cursing under his breath, an angry scowl on his face, he trotted off after Diane.

Reva and Pam stepped away from their hiding place. "It didn't work," Pam whispered glumly.

Reva chewed her bottom lip. "Who *told* those idiots to fix the elevator? Couldn't they leave it broken?" she fumed.

"Now what?" Pam asked, her voice trembling. She raised her hand and gently touched the purple welt on her cheek.

"I—I don't know," Reva stammered, frozen in fright.

"They went back to the toy department," Pam said, turning her glance down the long center aisle. "So maybe we do have time to take the elevator down." She stepped forward and pressed the button.

"Maybe," Reva replied tensely. She raised her eyes to the floor indicator above the two elevators. "It went all the way back to one."

Pam jammed her finger on the button again. And again.

"That won't make it come any faster," Reva whispered. She turned back toward the toy department. "Shh. I hear them. Oh, no! I think they're coming back!"

Pam frantically pushed the black elevator button. "Hurry. Hurry. Oh, please—hurry!"

They both watched the arrow above the elevators move slowly up. Two . . . three . . .

"It's Pres and Diane!" Pam cried. "They're going to catch us!"

Four . . . five!

The elevator door on the left started to slide open.

Reva glanced behind them. Pres and Diane were running down the center aisle toward them.

"Hurry!" Reva cried, pushing Pam toward the opening elevator door.

Pam stumbled forward. Then stopped.

"Oh!" Reva cried out as a man in the elevator stepped toward them, blocking the door, blocking their escape.

She recognized him at once. She recognized the blue sunglasses, the black trench coat.

The man who had followed her at the mall.

He raised his black-gloved hand and pointed a small dark pistol at Reva.

Chapter 35

"YOU'RE COMING WITH ME"

His eyes hidden behind the cold blue glasses, his face set in a hard frown, the man moved quickly out of the elevator.

Pam shrank back. A confused cry escaped her lips. When she saw the gun in the man's hand, her mouth dropped open in alarm.

Reva sighed loudly and prepared to surrender. He's working with Pres, Diane, and Danny, she realized. That's why he was following me Saturday afternoon.

But to her surprise, the man pushed past her.

He raised the pistol and called to Pres and Diane, who stood frozen in the aisle, several yards away, startled expressions on their faces.

"Stop right there! FBI!" the man called.

Reva and Pam cast dumbfounded looks at each other.

The FBI? Reva thought. He's *not* working with the kidnappers? He's an FBI agent?

How did he know where to find us?

"Get down, girls," the FBI agent ordered, waving them down with his free hand. Then he took off after Pres and Diane.

The two kidnappers turned and ran, disappearing into the toy department. Reva heard a loud crash. Someone had collided with one of the displays.

"Stop right there!" she heard the agent shout to them. "You can't get out! I have backup downstairs!" He disappeared around a corner.

Reva heard more footsteps. Angry shouts.

"I—I can't believe it," Pam exclaimed with a shudder of relief. "We're—we're going to be okay."

"But how did he know we were up here?" Reva demanded.

"It doesn't matter," Pam said, throwing her arms around her cousin's shoulders. "We're okay. We're okay now." She pressed her hot face against Reva's cheek. "I'm so sorry, Reva. Really, I'm so sorry," she said, sobbing.

"Pam—please—my arm!" Reva cried, recoiling from the pain.

"Oh. Sorry." Pam took a step back, wiping her eyes with her fingers. "I'm just so happy it's over and we're okay."

"What's over?" a stern voice demanded.

Reva and Pam both spun around to see Danny

standing in the aisle. His eyes burned angrily from one of them to the other. He was breathing hard, his stomach heaving up and down. His black hair was wet and matted to his forehead.

He raised the silver pistol. "You're coming with me," he said through clenched teeth.

He jammed his finger hard on the elevator button and held it, keeping the pistol poised on Reva and Pam.

"Don't try anything," Danny warned. "I'll use this gun. I really will."

"Please—" Pam started.

"Shut up!" he shouted, his features tight with fury. "This wasn't my idea, you know. I just wanted a little extra spending money, that's all."

"Please—" Pam repeated her plea.

"That's all I wanted. A little extra for Christmas," Danny growled. "You're not going to ruin it! Just shut up—and move! You're coming with me!"

Chapter 36

A SCREAM

"Let's go," Danny ordered. He gave Reva a hard shove toward the elevator.

Reva cried out from the paralyzing pain that bolted up from her broken arm.

The elevator door on the right slid open.

Still convulsed in pain, Reva turned in time to see Pam make a grab for the pistol.

"Hey—!" Danny cried out angrily, jerking the gun from Pam's grasp.

With a loud shriek Pam snatched at Danny's arm, pulled it behind him, grabbed at his waist.

"I'll kill you! I'll really kill you!" Danny screamed.

He and Pam were down on the floor now, wrestling, hitting each other, uttering sharp cries of pain and fury, twisting over each other.

"Ohh!" Pam groaned as she made another frantic grab for the pistol.

Danny drove his fist toward Pam's jaw, and missed. Pam held on.

"I've got it!" Pam cried. Sprawled on top of Danny, she held up the pistol, then tried to toss it to Reva.

But Danny reached a hand up and batted the gun away. It clattered over the floor, sliding to a stop at the foot of a display case.

With a desperate cry Pam scrambled to her feet and dove for the gun.

"Keep it!" Danny cried breathlessly. "I'm out of here!"

With a loud groan he jumped up quickly and lumbered into the open elevator.

Reva shut her eyes tight. She heard Danny scream all the way down.

The scream ended four floors below in a sickening *splat.*

It was a sound Reva knew she would never forget.

Chapter 37

"SILENT NIGHT"

Pam slumped against the display case, the gun dangling from her hand. She raised her eyes to Reva, her face white with horror. "Wh-what happened?"

"The elevator on the right," Reva murmured, pointing. "It wasn't fixed, I guess. The doors shouldn't have opened. The elevator car was still on the first floor. Only the one on the left was fixed. Only the one on the left." She took a deep breath, hearing the sound of Danny's scream repeat in her mind.

The gun dropped from Pam's hand and clattered to the floor. Neither girl made any attempt to pick it up.

Pam stared blankly at Reva, as if not understanding what had just happened, as if not *wanting* to understand or believe it.

"It's my fault," Pam murmured.

"No." Reva stepped forward to put a comforting arm around her cousin's trembling shoulders. "No, Pam. You may have saved our lives. He wanted to kill us. You were brave, Pam. You really were."

Pam lowered her eyes and didn't reply.

The elevator on the left opened, startling them both. Four FBI agents in dark coats, their revolvers drawn, burst out, their faces tense and alert.

"Are you okay?" one of them asked Reva.

"Define *okay,"* Reva replied.

Pam snickered and squeezed Reva's hand. "Same old Reva," she said.

In a short while the agents returned with Pres and Diane in handcuffs. Pres received the news about Danny in silent horror. He flinched, his entire body jolting as if hit by an electric current. But he didn't utter a sound.

"No happy ending," Diane muttered bitterly as she and Pres were taken away.

The man in the blue sunglasses introduced himself as Agent Barkley. "We have to get you both to a hospital," he said solemnly. "We'll radio for your parents to meet you there."

A few minutes later Reva and Pam sat in the back of the large gray FBI car as Agent Barkley drove to Shadyside General.

"I just don't understand how you knew where to find us," Reva said.

Agent Barkley turned to flash her a modest smile.

"Some of it was modern technology. Some of it was luck," he replied.

"Huh? Come on. Tell me," Reva insisted.

"Your phone in the house has a number revealer on it," Barkley explained. "You know. The readout that identifies the phone number of the person calling."

"Yeah. We got it from the phone company a few months ago," Reva said.

"Well," the agent continued, "when the kidnapper phoned your father to ask for the ransom money, the phone number of the store flashed on. So we knew right away that they were holding you at the department store."

"But it's a big store," Reva said. "We could've been anywhere in it."

"That's where the luck part came in," Barkley replied. "The other agents and I came in through the back of the store. We had no idea where they were keeping you. We split up and started to search. And then I saw the employee elevator start to move. I just happened to be in the right place at the right time. I watched it stop on five. I knew that had to be it."

He turned into the hospital lot entrance and headed the car toward the emergency room. "I rode the elevator to five—and there you were," he said. "Sometimes we get lucky."

Reva groaned from a stab of pain in her shoulder. "Yeah. This is my lucky day," she said, rolling her eyes.

The car stopped. The agent jumped out to help the girls out of the back.

Reva's dad and Pam's parents were waiting by the emergency room door. They came running eagerly.

Hugs and tears.

And then another car pulled up, its headlights sweeping over all of them. Victor came running out, leaving the car door open and the engine running.

At first Reva thought he was rushing to greet her. But when he ran to Pam, grabbing her in his arms, sweeping her up in an emotional hug, Reva found herself feeling relieved.

A happy ending for all, she thought with a sigh. She followed everyone into the hospital.

Stepping into the bright glare of the waiting room, Reva stopped. What was that song, that song on the speaker above the reception desk?

It was "Silent Night."

"Silent Night." Of course.

About the Author

"Where do you get your ideas?"

That's the question that R. L. Stine is asked most often. "I don't know where my ideas come from," he says. "But I do know that I have a lot more scary stories in my mind that I can't wait to write."

So far, he has written nearly three dozen mysteries and thrillers for young people, all of them bestsellers.

Bob grew up in Columbus, Ohio. Today he lives in an apartment near Central Park in New York City with his wife, Jane, and fourteen-year-old son, Matt.

The Nightmares
Never End . . .
When You Visit

Next . . . *THE NEW BOY*

Handsome, mysterious Ross Gabriel is new to Shadyside High, and all the girls are after him for a date. Janie, Eve and Faith make a bet to see which one will be lucky enough to go out with Ross first.

But soon the girls discover that a date with Ross ends not with the usual goodnight kiss, but in gruesome death. Janie doesn't feel lucky anymore—her dream date has turned into a fatal nightmare!